"I just wanted to see you," Maddy said.

"Look, I'm lousy at this sort of thing," she continued. "I never had time to develop a lot of style, and I only say clever lines when they're fed to me. I wanted to see you." Defiantly, she sat down on the sofa. "So I came."

"No style?" It amazed Reed that he could be amused when this unwanted need for Maddy was knotting his gut. "I see." He sat as well, careful to keep a full cushion between them. "Did you come to proposition me?"

Temper flared in her eyes. "I see entertainers don't have a patent on ego. I suppose the women you're used to are ready to tumble into bed when you crook your finger."

The smile threatened again as he lifted his brandy. "The women I'm used to don't sing duets in the lobby with the security guard."

Dear Reader,

We at Silhouette **Special Edition** are very pleased to bring you this complete collector's set of *THE O'HURLEYS!* by award-winning Nora Roberts.

Just as each O'Hurley family member is a unique individual—Abby, Maddy, Chantel and Trace—so, too, does each of these four enchanting volumes stand alone on its own merits. Together, however, they create a complex, compelling family portrait, now completed with the appearance of *Without a Trace* (Silhouette **Special Edition** #625).

You won't want to miss a single member—or a single moment—so look for all four volumes: *The Last Honest Woman*, *Dance to the Piper*, *Skin Deep* and now, *Without a Trace*. Meet *THE O'HURLEYS!*, united at last. We think you'll be glad you did.

Best wishes,

The Editors

NORA ROBERTS
Dance to the Piper

Silhouette Special Edition
Published by Silhouette Books New York
America's Publisher of Contemporary Romance

For my brother Bill.
Thanks for taking me backstage.

SILHOUETTE BOOKS
300 East 42nd St., New York, N.Y. 10017

ISBN: 0-373-48232-9

First Silhouette Books printing July 1988
Second Silhouette Books printing October 1990

Printed in the U.S.A.

NORA ROBERTS

is one of Silhouette Books' most popular and prolific authors. She has written for the Silhouette Romance, Silhouette Special Edition and Silhouette Intimate Moments lines, as well as contributing stories to *Silhouette Christmas Stories 1986* and to the 1989 *Silhouette Summer Sizzler.*

When we published the four-book MacGregor Series, readers wrote in requesting the parents' story—and Nora Roberts responded by writing *For Now, Forever.* When we published the fifth MacGregor book, we reissued the first four. When Nora Roberts wrote THE O'HURLEYS! about triplet sisters, readers clamored for the story of their elusive older brother. Silhouette Books is pleased to present *Without a Trace,* along with reissuing *The Last Honest Woman, Dance to the Piper* and *Skin Deep.* When Silhouette asked Nora to comment on the miniseries, she said:

"Writing interlocking stories is always a pleasure. I get such a kick out of discovering what happened to the characters once their particular book closed! With the O'Hurleys, I discovered a family I could admire, a family I could laugh with and hurt for. I'm glad I had the chance to know them, and I hope that you'll feel the same way."

And for MacGregor fans, look for a collection of historical Christmas stories in November for a look at the early MacGregor clan.

THE O'HURLEYS!
Book Two: Maddy's Story

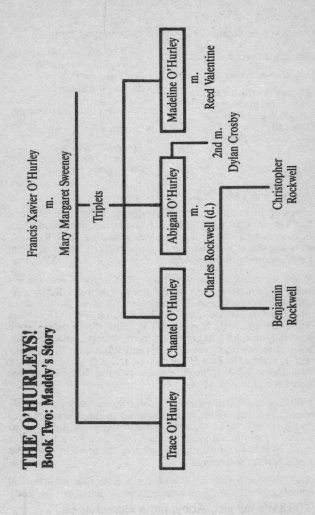

Francis Xavier O'Hurley
m.
Mary Margaret Sweeney

Triplets

Trace O'Hurley

Chantel O'Hurley

Abigail O'Hurley
m.
Charles Rockwell (d.)
2nd m.
Dylan Crosby

Madeline O'Hurley
m.
Reed Valentine

Benjamin Rockwell

Christopher Rockwell

Prologue

During the break between lunch and cocktails, the club was empty. The floors were scarred but clean enough, and the paint on the walls was only a little dull from fighting with cigarette smoke. There was the scent intrinsic to such places—old liquor and stale perfume mixed with coffee that was no longer fresh. To a certain type of person it was as much home as a cozy fire and plump cushions. The O'Hurleys made their home wherever audiences gathered.

When the after-dinner crowd strolled in, the lights would be dimmed, and it wouldn't look so grimy. Now, strong sunlight shone through the two small windows and lighted the dust and dents mercilessly. The mirror in back of a bar lined with bottles spread some of the light around but reflected mostly on the small stage in the center of the room.

"That's my girl, Abby, put a nice smile on."

Frank O'Hurley took his five-year-old triplets through the short dance routine he wanted to add to the show that night, demonstrating the prissy moves with his wiry body. They were playing a family hotel at a nice, reasonably priced resort in the Poconos. He figured the audience would have a soft spot for three little girls.

"I wish you'd time your brainstorms better, Frank." His wife, Molly, sat at a corner table, hurriedly sewing bows on the white dresses her daughters would wear in a few hours. "I'm not a bloody seamstress, you know."

"You're a trouper, Molly my love, and the best thing that ever happened to Frank O'Hurley."

"There's nothing truer than that," she muttered, but smiled to herself.

"All right, my darlings, let's try it again." He smiled at the three little angels God had blessed him with in one fell swoop. If the Lord saw fit to present him with three babies for the price of one, Frank figured the Lord was entitled to a sense of humor.

Chantel was already a beauty, with a round cherub's face and dark blue eyes. He winked at her, knowing she was more interested in the bows on the dress she'd wear than in the routine. Abby was all amiability. She'd dance because her pop wanted her to and because it would be fun to be onstage with her sisters. Frank urged her to smile again and demonstrated the curtsy he wanted.

Maddy, with an elfin face and hair already hinting toward red, mimicked his move perfectly, her eyes never leaving his. Frank felt his heart swell with love for the three of them. He laid his hand on his son's shoulder.

"Give us a two-bar intro, Trace, my boy. A snappy one."

Trace obligingly ran his fingers over the keys. It was Frank's regret he couldn't afford lessons for the boy. What Trace knew of playing he'd learned from watching and listening. Music rang out, jumpy and bright.

"How's that, Pop?"

"You're a pistol." Frank rubbed a hand over Trace's head. "Okay, girls, let's take it from the top."

He worked them another fifteen minutes, patiently, making them giggle at their mistakes. The five-minute routine would be far from perfect, but he was shrewd enough to recognize the charm of it. They'd expand the act bit by bit as they went on. It was the off-season at the resort now, but if they made a bit of a mark they'd secure a return engagement. Life for Frank was made up of gigs and return engagements. He saw no reason his family shouldn't be of the same mind.

Still, the minute he saw Chantel losing interest he broke off, knowing her sisters wouldn't be far behind.

"Wonderful." He bent to give each of them a smacking kiss, as generous with affection as he'd have liked to be with money. "We're going to knock them dead."

"Is our name going on the poster?" Chantel demanded, and Frank roared with delighted laughter.

"Want billing, do you, my little pigeon? Hear that, Molly?"

"Doesn't surprise me." She set down her sewing to rest her fingers.

"Tell you what, Chantel, you get billing when you can do this." He started a slow, deceptively simple tap routine, holding a hand out to his wife. Smiling, Molly rose to join him. A dozen years of dancing together had them moving in unison from the first step.

Abby slid onto the piano bench beside Trace and watched. He began to improvise a silly little tune that made Abby smile.

"Chantel's going to practice till she can do it," he murmured.

Abby smiled up at him. "Then we'll all get our names on the poster."

"I can show you how," he whispered, listening to his parents' feet strike the wooden stage.

"Will you show us all how?"

As an old man of ten, Trace was amused by the way his little sisters stuck together. He'd have gotten the same response from any of them. "I just might."

Content, she settled back against his shoulder. Her parents were laughing, enjoying the exertion, the rhythm. It seemed to Abby that her parents were always laughing. Even when her mother got that cross look on her face, Pop would make her laugh. Chantel was watching, her eyes narrowed, experimenting a bit but not quite catching the movements. She'd get mad, Abby knew. But when she got mad, she made sure she got what she wanted.

"I want to do it," Maddy said from the corner of the stage.

Frank laughed. With his arms around Molly's waist, the two of them circled the stage, feet tapping, sliding, shuffling. "Do you now, little turnip?"

"I *can* do it," she told him, and with a stubborn look on her face she began to tap her feet—heel, toe, toe, heel—until she was moving center stage.

Caught off balance, Frank stopped on a dime, and Molly bumped heavily into him. "Look at that, will you, Molly."

Pushing her hair out of her eyes, Molly watched her youngest daughter struggling to capture the basics of their tap routine. And she was doing it. She felt a mixture of pride and regret only a mother would understand. "Looks like we'll be buying another set of taps, Frank."

"That it does." Frank felt twice the pride and none of the regret. He released his wife to concentrate on his daughter. "No, try this now." He took the moves slowly. Hop, shuffle, stamp. Brush, step, brush, step, and step to the side. He took Maddy's hand and, careful to keep his steps small to match hers, moved again. She moved right with him.

"Now this." His excitement growing, he looked at his son. "Give me a downbeat. Listen to the count, Maddy. One and two and three and four. Tap. No body weight here. Toe stab front, then back. Now a riff." Again he demonstrated, and again she imitated the steps.

"We'll put it all together now and end with a step slide, arms like this, see?" He brought his arms out to the side in a sharp, glitzy move, then winked at her. "You're going to sell it."

"Sell it," she repeated, frowning in concentration.

"Give us the count, Trace." Frank took her hand again, feeling the pleasure build as she moved in unison with him. "We've got ourselves a dancer here, Molly!" Frank hefted Maddy into his arms and let her fly. She squealed, not because she feared he wouldn't catch her but because she knew he would.

The sensation of dropping through the air was every bit as thrilling as the dance itself had been. She wanted more.

Chapter One

Five, six, seven, eight!

Twenty-four feet hit the wooden floor in unison. The echo was wonderful. Twelve bodies twisted, swooped and plunged as one. Mirrors threw their images right back at them. Arms flowed out on signal, legs lifted, heads tilted, turned, then fell back.

Sweat rolled. And the scent was the theater.

The piano banged out notes, and the melody swelled in the old rehearsal hall. Music had echoed there before, feet had responded, heartbeats had raced and muscles had ached. It would happen again and again, year after year, for as long as the building stood.

Many stars had rehearsed in that room. Show-business legends had polished routines on the same boards. Countless unknown and unremembered line dancers had worked there until their muscles had gone stringy with fatigue. It was a Broadway that the paying public rarely saw.

The assistant choreographer, his glasses fogging a bit in the steamy heat, clapped out the beat constantly as he shouted the moves. Beside him the choreographer, the man who had sculpted the dance, stood watching with eyes as dark and alert as a bird's.

"Hold it!"

The piano music stopped. Movement stopped. The dancers drooped with a combination of exhaustion and relief.

"It drags there."

Drags?

The dancers, still a unit, rolled their eyes and tried to ignore their aching muscles. The choreographer studied them, then gave the signal to take five. Twelve bodies dropped against the wall, shifting together so that heads fell on convenient shoulders or abdomens. Calves were massaged. Feet flexed, relaxed, and flexed again. They talked little. Breath was an important commodity, to be hoarded whenever possible. Beneath them, the floor was battle-scarred, covered with masking tape that had set the marks for dozens of other shows. But there was only one show that mattered now: this one.

"Want a bite?"

Maddy O'Hurley roused herself to look down at the chocolate bar. She considered it, coveted it, then shook her head. One bite would never be enough. "No, thanks. Sugar makes me light-headed when I'm dancing."

"I need a lift." The woman, her skin as dark and rich as the candy, took a huge bite. "Like now. All that guy needs is a whip and a chain."

Maddy glanced over at the choreographer as he bent over the accompanist. "He's tough. We'll be glad we've got him before this is over."

"Yeah, but right now I'd like to—"

"Strangle him with some piano wire?" Maddy suggested, and was rewarded with a quick, husky laugh.

"Something like that."

Her energy was coming back, and she could feel herself drying off. The room smelled of sweat and the fruity splash-on many of the dancers used to combat it. "I've seen you at auditions," Maddy commented. "You're real good."

"Thanks." The woman carefully wrapped the rest of the candy and slipped it into her dance bag. "Wanda Starre—two *r*s and an *e*."

"Maddy O'Hurley."

"Yeah, I know." Maddy's name was already well-known in the theater district. The gypsies—the dancers who wandered from show to show, job to job— knew her as one of their own who'd made it. Woman to woman, dancer to dancer, Wanda recognized Maddy as someone who hadn't forgotten her roots. "It's my first white contract," she said in an undertone.

"No kidding?" White contracts were for principals, pink for chorus. There was much, much more to it than color coding. Surprised, Maddy straightened to get a better look. The woman beside her had a large-featured, exotic face and the long, slender neck and strong shoulders of a dancer. Her body was longer than Maddy's. Even sprawled on the floor, Maddy gauged a five-inch difference from shoulder to toe.

"Your first time out of chorus?"

"That's right." Wanda glanced at the other dancers relaxing and recharging. "I'm scared to death."

Maddy toweled off her face. "Me, too."

"Come on. You've already starred in a hit."

"I haven't starred in this one yet. And I haven't worked with Macke." She watched the choreographer, still wiry at sixty, move away from the piano. "Show time," she murmured. The dancers rose and listened to the next set of instructions.

For another two hours they moved, absorbed, strove and polished. When the other dancers were dismissed, Maddy was given a ten-minute break, then came back to go through her solo. As lead she would dance with the chorus, perform solo and dance with the male lead and the other principals. She would prepare for the play in much the same way an athlete prepared for a marathon. Practice, discipline and more practice. In a show that was slated to run two hours and ten minutes, she would be on stage about two-thirds of the time. Dance routines would be absorbed into the memory banks of her mind, muscles and limbs. Everything would have to respond in sync at the call of the downbeat.

"Try it with your arms out, shoulder-level," Macke instructed. "Ball change before the kicks and keep the energy up."

The assistant choreographer gave the count, and Maddy threw herself into a two-minute routine that would have left a linebacker panting.

"Better." From Macke, Maddy knew that was praise indeed. "This time, keep your shoulders loose." He walked over and laid his blunt, ugly hands on Maddy's damp shoulders. "After the turn, angle stage left. I want the moves sharp; don't follow through, cut them off. You're a stripper, not a ballerina.''

She smiled at him because while he was criticizing her he was massaging the exhausted muscles of her shoulders. Macke had a reputation for being a grueling instructor, but he had the soul of a dancer. "I'll try to remember that."

She took the count again and let her body do the thinking. Sharp, sassy, acerbic. That was what the part called for, so that was what she'd be. When she couldn't use her voice to get into the part, she had to use her body. Her legs lifted, jackknifing from the knee in a series of hitch kicks. Her arms ranged out to the side, contracted to cuddle her body and flew up, while her feet moved by memory to the beat.

Her short, smooth crop of reddish-blond hair flopped around a sweatband that was already soaked. She'd have the added weight of a wildly curled shoulder-length wig for this number, but she refused to think about that. Her face glowed like wet porcelain, but none of the effort showed. Her features were small, almost delicate, but she knew how to use her whole face to convey an expression, an emotion. It was often necessary to overconvey in the theater. Moisture beaded on her soft upper lip, but she smiled, grinned, laughed and grimaced as the mood of the dance demanded.

Without makeup her face was attractive—or cute, as Maddy had wearily come to accept—with its triangular shape, elfin features and wide, brandy-colored eyes. For the part of Mary Howard, alias the Merry Widow, Maddy would rely on the expertise of the makeup artist to turn her into something slick and sultry. For now she depended on her own gift for expression and movement to convey the character of the overexperienced stripper looking for an easy way out.

In some ways, she thought, she'd been preparing all her life for this part—the train and bus rides with her family, traveling from town to town and club to club to entertain for union scale and a meal. By the age of five she'd been able to gauge an audience. Were they hostile, were they laid-back, were they receptive? Knowing the audience's mood could mean the difference between success and failure. Maddy had discovered early how to make subtle changes in a routine to draw the best response. Her life, from the time she could walk, had been played out onstage. In twenty-six years she'd never regretted a moment of it.

There had been classes, endless classes. Though the names and faces of her teachers had blurred, every movement, every position, every step was firmly lodged in her mind. When there hadn't been the time or money for a formal class, her father had been there, setting up a makeshift *barre* in a motel room to put his children through practice routines and exercises.

She'd been born a gypsy, coming into the world with her two sisters when her parents had been on the way to a performance. Becoming a Broadway gypsy had been inevitable. She'd auditioned, failed, and dealt with the misery of disappointment. She'd auditioned, succeeded, and dealt with the fear of opening night. Because of her nature and her background, she'd never had to deal with a lack of confidence.

For six years she'd struggled on her own, without the cushion of her parents, her brother and her sisters. She'd danced in chorus lines and taken classes. Between rehearsals she'd waited tables to help pay for the instructions that never ended and the dance shoes that wore out too soon. She'd broken through to principal, but had continued to study. She'd made second lead, but never gave up her classes. She finally stopped waiting tables.

Her biggest part had been the lead in *Suzanna's Park*, a plum she'd relished until she'd felt she'd sucked it dry. Leaving it had been a risk, but there was enough gypsy in her to have made the move an adventure.

Now she was playing the role of Mary, and the part was harder, more complex and more demanding than anything that had come before. She was going to work for Mary just as hard as she would make Mary work for her.

When the music ended, Maddy stood in the center of the hall, hands on hips, labored breathing echoing off the walls. Her body begged to be allowed to collapse, but if Macke had signaled, she would have revved up and gone on.

"Not bad, kid." He tossed her a towel.

With a little laugh, Maddy buried her face in it. The cloth was no longer fresh, but it still absorbed moisture. "Not bad? You know damn well it was terrific."

"It was good." Macke's lips twitched; Maddy knew that was as good as a laugh, for him. "Can't stand cocky dancers." But he watched her towel off, pleased and grateful that there was such a furnace of energy in her compact body. She was his tool, his canvas. His success would depend on her ability as much as hers did on his.

Maddy slung the towel around her neck as she walked over to the piano where the accompanist was already stacking up the score. "Can I ask you something, Macke?"

"Shoot." He drew out a cigarette; it was a habit Maddy looked on with mild pity.

"How many musicals have you done now? Altogether, I mean, dancing and choreographing?"

"Lost count. We'll call it plenty."

"Okay." She accepted his answer easily, though she would have bet her best tap shoes that he knew the exact number. "How do you gauge our chances with this one?"

"Nervous?"

"No. Paranoid."

He took two short drags. "It's good for you."

"I don't sleep well when I'm paranoid. I need my rest."

His lips twitched again. "You've got the best—me. You've got a good score, a catchy libretto and a solid book. What do you want?"

"Standing room only." She accepted a glass of water from the assistant choreographer and sipped carefully.

He answered because he respected her. It wasn't based on what she'd done in *Suzanna's Park*; rather, he admired what she and others like her did every day. She was twenty-six and had been dancing for more than twenty years. "You know who's backing us?"

With a nod, she sipped again, letting the water play in her mouth, not cold but wonderfully wet. "Valentine Records."

"Got any idea why a record company would negotiate to be the only backer of a musical?"

"Exclusive rights to the cast album."

"You catch on." He crushed out the cigarette, wishing immediately for another. He only thought of them when the music wasn't playing—on the piano, or in his head. Luckily for his lungs, that wasn't often. "Reed Valentine's our angel, a second-generation corporate bigwig, and from what I'm told he's tougher than his old man ever thought of being. He's not interested in us, sweetheart. He's interested in making a profit."

"That's fair enough," Maddy decided after a moment. "I'd like to see him make one." She grinned. "A big one."

"Good thinking. Hit the shower."

The pipes were noisy and the water sprayed in staccato bursts, but it was cool and wet. Maddy propped both forearms against the wall and let the stream pour over her head. She'd taken a ballet class early that morning. From there she'd come directly to the rehearsal hall, first to go over two of the songs with the composer. The singing didn't worry her—she had a clean voice, excellent pitch and a good range. Most of all, she was loud. The theater didn't tolerate stingy voices.

She'd spent her formative years as one of the O'Hurley Triplets. When you sang in bars and clubs with faulty acoustics and undependable audio equipment, you learned to be generous with your lungs.

She had a pretty good handle on her lines. Tomorrow she'd be rehearsing with the other actors—after jazz class and before dance rehearsal. The acting itself gave her a few flutters. Chantel was the true actor in the family, just as Abby had the most fluid voice.

Maddy would rely on the character of Mary to pull her through.

Her heart was in the dancing. It had to be. There was nothing more strenuous, more demanding, more exhausting. It had caught her—mind, body and soul—from the moment her father had taught her her first simple tap routine in a dingy little lounge in Pennsylvania.

Look at me now, Pop, she thought as she shut off the inconsistent spray. I'm on Broadway.

Maddy toweled off quickly to avoid a chill and dressed in the street clothes she'd stuffed in her dance bag.

The big hall echoed. The composer and lyricist were performing minor surgery on one of their own tunes. There would be changes tomorrow, changes she and the other vocalists would have to learn. That was nothing new. Macke would have a dozen subtle alterations to the number they'd just gone over. That was nothing new, either.

Maddy heard the sound of dance shoes hitting the floor. The rhythm repeated over and over. Someone from the chorus was vocalizing. The vowel sounds rose and fell melodically.

Maddy swung her bag over her shoulders and descended the stairs to the street door with one thing on her mind—food. The energy and calories that she'd drained after a full day of exercise had to be replenished—but replenished wisely. She'd trained herself long ago to look at a dish of yogurt and a banana split with the same enthusiasm. Tonight it would be yogurt, garnished with fresh fruit and joined by a big bowl of barley soup and spinach salad.

At the door she paused a moment and listened again. The vocalist was still doing scales; piano music drifted, tinny and slight with distance. Feet slapped the floor in rhythm. The sounds were as much a part of her as her own heartbeat.

God bless Reed Valentine, she decided, and stepped out into the balmy dusk.

She'd taken about two steps when a sharp jerk on her dance bag sent her spinning around. He was hardly more than a boy, really—sixteen, seventeen—but she couldn't miss the hard, desperate look in his eye. She'd been desperate a few times herself.

"You should be in school," she told him as they began a tug-of-war over her bag.

She'd looked like a pushover. A hundred pounds of fluff to be tossed aside while he took the bag and fled. Her strength surprised him but made him all the more determined to have whatever cash and plastic she carried. In the dim light beside the stairs of the old building, no one noticed the struggle. She thought of screaming, then thought of how young he was and tried reason instead. It had been pointed out to her once or twice that not everyone wanted to be reformed. That never stopped her from trying.

"You know what's in here?" she asked him as they pulled and tugged on the canvas. He was running out of breath more quickly than she was. "Sweaty tights and a towel that's already molding. And my ballet shoes."

Remembering them, she held on tighter. A pro, she knew, would have given up and looked for an easier mark. The boy was beginning to call her all sorts of names, but she ignored them, believing that he was entitled. "They're almost new, but they won't do you any good," she continued in the same rational tone. "I need them a lot more than you do." As they scuffled, she banged her heel against the iron railing and swore. She could afford to lose a few dollars, but she couldn't afford an injury. So he didn't want to be reformed, but maybe he'd compromise.

"Look, if you'll let go a minute I'll give you half of the cash I have. I don't want to have to bother changing my credit cards—which I'll do by calling that 800 number the minute you take off. I don't have time to replace the shoes, and I need them tomorrow. All the cash," she decided as she heard the seam in her bag begin to give. "I think I have about thirty dollars."

He gave a fierce tug that sent Maddy stumbling forward. Then, at the sound of a shout, he released his hold. The bag dropped like a stone, its contents tumbling out. The boy, not wasting time on a curse, ran like a rocket down the street and around the first corner. Muttering to herself, Maddy crouched down to gather up her belongings.

"Are you all right?"

She reached for her tattered leg warmer and saw a pair of highly polished Italian shoes. As a dancer, she took a special notice of what people wore on their feet. Shoes often reflected one's personality and self-esteem. Polished Italian shoes meant wealth and appreciation for what wealth could provide to Maddy. Above the exquisite leather were pale gray trousers that fell precisely to the middle of the foot, their creases perfectly aligned. An organized, sensible man, she decided as she gathered the loose change that had spilled from the bottom of her bag.

Looking higher, she saw that the trousers fit well over narrow hips and were buckled by a thin belt with a small, intricately worked gold buckle. Stylish, but not trendy.

The jacket was open, revealing a trim waist, a long torso smoothed by a light blue shirt and a darker tie. All silk. Maddy approved highly of silk worn against the body. Luxuries were only luxuries if they were enjoyed.

She looked at the hand that reached down to help her up. It was tanned, with long, attractive fingers. On his wrist was a gold watch that looked both expensive and practical. She put her hand in his and felt heat and strength and, she thought, impatience.

"Thank you." She said it before she looked at his face. From her long visual journey up his body, she knew he was tall and lean. Rangy, not in the way of a dancer but in the way of a man who knew discipline without the extremes of sacrifice. In the same interested way she'd studied him from shoes to shoulders, she studied his face.

He was clean-shaven, and every line and plane showed clearly. His cheeks were slightly hollow, giving his otherwise hard and stern look a poetic hint. She'd always had a soft spot for poets. His mouth was in a firm line now, signalling disapproval or annoyance, while below it was a trace, just a touch, of a cleft in his chin. His nose was straight, aristocratic, and though he looked down it at her, she took no offense. The eyes were a dark, flinty gray, and they conveyed as clearly as words the message that he didn't care to waste time rescuing damsels in distress.

The fact that he didn't, and yet had, made Maddy warm toward him.

He brushed his fingers through his burnished blond hair and stared back at her and wondered if she was going into shock. "Sit down," he told her in the quick, clipped voice of a man accustomed to giving orders and having them obeyed. Immediately.

"I'm okay," she said, sending him an easy smile. He noticed for the first time that her face wasn't flushed or pale, that her eyes weren't mirroring fear. She didn't fit his picture of a woman who'd nearly been mugged. "I'm glad you came along when you did. That kid wasn't listening to reason."

She bent down again to gather her things. He told himself he should go and leave her to pick up her own scattered belongings, but instead he took a deep breath, checked his watch, then crouched down to help her. "Do you always try to reason with muggers?"

"Apprentice mugger would be my guess." She found her key ring where it had bounced into a deep crack in the sidewalk. "And I was trying to negotiate."

He held up Maddy's oldest practice tights, gingerly, by the backs of the knees. "Do you really think this was worth negotiating over?"

"Absolutely." She took them from him, rolled them up and stuffed them in her bag.

"He could have hurt you."

"He could have gotten my shoes." Maddy picked up her ballet slippers and stroked the supple leather. "A fat lot of good they'd have done him, and I only bought them three weeks ago. Hand me that sweatband, would you?"

He retrieved it, then grimaced. Dangling it by his fingertips, he handed it over. "Shower with this, do you?"

Laughing, she took it and dropped it in with the rest of her practice clothes. "No, it's just sweat. Sorry."

But there was no apology in her eyes, only humor. "Dressed like that, you don't look as though you'd recognize the substance."

"I don't generally carry it around in a bag with me." He wondered why he didn't simply move by her and start on his way. He was already five minutes late, but something about the way she continued to look up at him with such frank good humor kept him there. "You don't react like a woman who very nearly lost a pair of tights, a faded leotard, a ratty towel, two pairs of shoes and five pounds of keys."

"The towel's not that ratty." Satisfied she'd found everything, Maddy closed her beg again. "And anyway, I didn't lose them."

"Most of the women I know wouldn't negotiate with a mugger."

Interested, she studied him again. He looked like a man who would know dozens of women, all elegant and intelligent. "What would they do?"

"Scream, I imagine."

"If I'd done that, he'd have my bag and I'd be out of breath." She dismissed the idea with a graceful shrug of strong shoulders. "Anyway, thanks." She offered her hand again, a delicate one, narrow and naked of jewelry. "I think white knights are lovely."

She was small and completely alone, and it was getting darker by the minute. His natural instinct for noninvolvement warred with his conscience. The resolution took the form of annoyance. "You shouldn't be walking around in this neighborhood after dark."

She laughed again, the sound bright, rich and amused. "This is my neighborhood. I only live about four blocks away. I told you the kid was green. No self-respecting mugger's going to look twice at a dancer. They know dancers are usually broke. But you—" She stepped back and took another long look. He was definitely worth taking the time to look twice. "You're another matter. Dressed like that, you 'd be better off carrying your watch and your wallet in your shorts."

"I'll keep that in mind."

Deciding one good turn deserved another, Maddy merely nodded. "Can I give you directions? You don't look as though you know your way around the lower forties."

Why had he been the one feeling responsible for her? In another minute that kid might have planted a fist in her face, but she didn't appear to have considered that. "No, thanks. I'm just going inside here."

"Here?" Maddy glanced over her shoulder at the ramshackle building that housed the rehearsal hall, then looked at him speculatively. "You're not a dancer." She said that positively. It wasn't that he didn't move well—from the little she had seen, he'd looked good. He simply wasn't a dancer. "And not an actor," she decided after only a brief mental debate. "And I'd swear...you aren't a musician, even though you've got good hands."

Every time he tried to walk away from her she drew him back. "Why not?"

"Too conservative," Maddy told him immediately, but not with scorn. "Absolutely too straight. I mean you're dressed like a lawyer or a banker or—" It struck her, clear as a bell. She positively beamed at him. "An angel."

He lifted a brow. "You see a halo?"

"No, I don't think you'd be willing to carry that kind of weight around. An angel," she repeated. "A backer. Valentine Records?"

Yet again, Maddy offered her hand. He took it and found himself simply holding it. "That's right. Reed Valentine."

"I'm Merry Widow."

He frowned. "I beg your pardon?"

"The stripper," she said, and watched his eyes narrow. She might have left it at that, just for the possible shock value, but then he *had* helped her out. "From *Take It Off*. The play you're backing." Delighted with him, she covered his hand with her free one. "Maddy O'Hurley."

This was Maddy O'Hurley? This compact little urchin with the crop of disheveled red-blond hair and the scrubbed face was the same powerhouse he'd watched in *Suzanna's Park*? She'd worn a long blond wig for that, an *Alice in Wonderland* look, and period costumes of the 1890s, but still... Her voice had boomed out, filling every crack in the theater. She'd danced with a frenzied, feverish energy that had awed a man who was very difficult to impress.

One of the reasons he'd been willing to back the play was Maddy O'Hurley. Now he was face-to-face with her and swamped with doubts.

"Madeline O'Hurley?"

"That's what it says on the contract."

"I've seen you perform, Miss O'Hurley. I didn't recognize you."

"Lights, costume, makeup." She shrugged it off. When there weren't footlights, she prized her anonymity and acknowledged her own unremarkable looks. She'd been born one of three—Chantel had gotten the heart-stopping beauty, Abby the warm loveliness, and she'd gotten cute. Maddy figured there were reasons for it, but she couldn't help being amused by Reed's cautious look. "Now you're disappointed," she concluded with a secret smile.

"I never said—"

"Of course, you wouldn't. You're much too polite. Don't worry, Mr. Valentine Records, I'll deliver. Any O'Hurley's a wise investment." She laughed at her own private joke. The streetlight behind them flickered on, signaling that night was coming, like it or not. "I guess you've got meetings inside."

"Ten minutes ago."

"Time's only important when you're on cue. You've got the checkbook, captain, you're in charge." Before she stepped out of his way, she gave him a friendly pat on the arm. "Listen, if you're around in a couple of days, come by rehearsals." She took a few steps, turned and walked backward, grinning at him. "You can watch me bump and grind. I'm good, Valentine. Real good." With a *pirouette*, she turned away, eating up the sidewalk with an easy jog.

In spite of a penchant for promptness, Reed continued to watch her until she disappeared around the corner. He shook his head and started up the stairs. Then he noticed a small round hairbrush. The temptation to leave it where it lay was strong. Curiosity was stronger. When Reed scooped it up he noticed that it carried the faintest scent of shampoo—something lemon-scented and fresh. He resisted the urge to sniff at it, and stuck it in his jacket pocket. Would a woman like that miss a hair brush? he wondered, then shrugged the thought away. He'd see that she got it back in any case.

He was bound to see Maddy O'Hurley again anyway, he told himself. It wouldn't hurt to do one more good deed.

Chapter Two

Nearly a week passed before Reed managed to schedule another visit to the rehearsal hall. He was able to justify the trip to himself as good business sense, but just barely. It had never been his intention to become directly involved with the play itself. Meetings with the producer and sessions with the accountants would have been enough to keep him informed. Reed understood balance sheets, ledgers and neatly formed columns better than he did the noises and the scents inside the decaying old building. But it never hurt to keep a tight rein on an investment—even if the investment involved an odd woman with a vivid smile.

He felt out of place. He was a twenty-minute cab ride from his offices, yet just as out of place in the rehearsal hall in his three-piece suit as he would have been on some remote island in the South Seas where the natives wore bones in their ears.

He would never have considered his life sheltered. In the course of his career he'd visited some seamy areas, dealt with people from varied backgrounds. But he lived uptown, where the restaurants were sedate and the view of the park out his apartment window was restful.

As he started up the stairs, Reed told himself it was natural curiosity that had brought him back. That, coupled with the simple matter of protecting his interests. Valentine Records had sunk a good chunk of capital into *Take It Off*, and he was responsible for Valentine Records. Still, he reached into his pocket and toyed with Maddy's hair brush. Going against his natural inclinations, he headed toward the sounds of music and talk.

In a room wrapped with mirrors, he found the dancers. They weren't the glittery, spangly chorus one paid to see on a Broadway stage, but a ragtag, dripping group of men and women in frayed tights. To him they were a helter-skelter mix of faded, damp leotards without any hint of the precision or uniformity expected of professionals. He felt uneasy for a moment as they stood, most of them with their hands on their hips, and stared at the small, thin man he knew was the choreographer.

"Let's have a little more steam, boys and girls," Macke instructed. "This is a strip joint, not a cotillion. We've got to sell sex and keep it good-natured. Wanda, I want a hesitation on the hip roll, then make it broader. Maddy, raise some blood pressure when you step up in the shimmy. Bend it from the waist."

He demonstrated, and Maddy watched, considered the move, then grinned at him. "I saw the design for my costume, Macke. If I bend over like that, the boys in the front row are going to get an anatomy lesson.''

Macke looked her over. "A small one, in your case.''

The dancers around her snorted and cackled. Maddy took the ribbing with a good-humored laugh as they moved back into position to take the count. They moved, with gusto, on eight.

Reed watched with steadily growing astonishment. Over a floor shiny with sweat, the dancers sprang to life. Legs flashed, hips rolled. Men and women found their partners in what seemed to be a riot of churning bodies. There were lifts, jumps, spins and the soft stamp of feet. From his vantage point he could see the exertion, the drip of perspiration, the deep, controlled breathing. Then Maddy stepped out, and he forgot the rest.

The leotard clung to every curve and line of her body, with the dark patches only accentuating her shape. Her legs, even in battered tights, seemed to go all the way to her waist. Slowly at first, with her hands at the tops of her hips, she moved forward, then right, then left, always following the rotation of her hips. He didn't hear the count being called now, but she did.

Her arm snaked across her body, then flew out. It didn't take much imagination to understand that she had tossed aside some article of clothing. She kicked up, so that for a moment her foot was over her head. Slowly, erotically, she ran her fingertips down her thigh as she lowered her leg.

The pace picked up, and so did her rhythm. She moved like a leopard, twisting, turning, sinuous and smooth. Then, as the dancers behind her went into an orgy of movement, she bent from the waist and used her shoulders to fascinate. A man broke from the group and grabbed her arm. With nothing more than the angle of her body, the placement of her head, she conveyed teasing, taunting acceptance. When the music ended, she was caught against him, arched backward. And his hand was clamped firmly on her bottom.

"Better," Macke decided. The dancers sagged, unwilling to waste energy by standing upright. Maddy and her partner seemed to collapse onto each other.

"Watch your hand, Jack."

"I am." He leaned over her shoulder just a little. "I've got my eye right on it."

She managed a breathless laugh before she pushed him away. For the first time, she saw Reed standing in the doorway. He looked every inch the proper, successful businessman. Because she'd wanted to see him again, had known she eventually would, Maddy sent him an uncomplicated, friendly smile.

"Take lunch," Macke announced as he lit a cigarette. "I want Maddy, Wanda and Terry back in an hour. Someone give Carter the word I want him, too. Chorus is due in room B at 1:30 for vocals."

The room was already emptying. Maddy took her towel and buried her face in it before she walked over to Reed. Several of the female dancers passed him with none-too-subtle invitations in their eyes.

"Hello again." Maddy slung her towel around her neck, then gently eased him out of the way of the hungry dancers. "Did you see the whole thing?"

"Whole thing?"

"The dance."

"Yes." He was having a hard time remembering anything but the way she had moved, the sensuality that had poured out of her.

With a laugh, she hung on to the ends of the towel and leaned against the wall. "And?"

"Impressive." Now she looked simply like a woman who'd been hard at work—attractive enough, but hardly primitively arousing. "You've, ah . . . a lot of energy, Miss O'Hurley."

"Oh, I'm packed with it. Are you here for another meeting?"

"No." Feeling a little foolish, he pulled out her hairbrush. "I think this is yours."

"Well, yeah." Pleased, Maddy took it from him. "I gave it up for lost. That was nice of you." She dabbed at her face with the towel again. "Hang on a minute." She walked away to stuff the brush and towel in her bag. Reed allowed himself the not-so-mild pleasure of watching her leotard stretch over her bottom as she bent over. She came back, slinging the bag over her shoulder.

"How about some lunch?" she asked him.

It was so casual, and so ridiculously appealing, that he nearly agreed. "I've got an appointment."

"Dinner?"

His brow lifted. She was looking up at him, a half smile on her lips and laughter in her eyes. The women he knew would have coolly left it to him to make the approach and the maneuvers. "Are you asking me for a date?"

The question rang with cautious politeness, and she had to laugh again. "You catch on fast, Valentine Records. Are you a carnivore?"

"I beg your pardon?"

"Do you eat meat?" she explained. "I know a lot of people who won't touch it."

"Ah . . . yes." He wondered why he should feel apologetic.

"Fine. I'll fix you a steak. Got a pen?"

Not certain whether he was amused or just dazed, Reed drew one out of his breast pocket.

"I knew you would." Maddy rattled off her address. "See you at seven." She called for someone down the hall to wait for her and dashed off before he could agree or refuse.

Reed walked out of the building without writing down her address. But he didn't forget it.

Maddy always did things on impulse. That was how she justified asking Reed to dinner when she barely knew him and didn't have anything in the house more interesting than banana yogurt. *He* was interesting, she told herself. So she stopped on the way home, after a full ten hours on her feet, and did some frenzied marketing.

It wasn't often she cooked. Not that she couldn't when push came to shove, it was simply that it was easier to eat out of a carton or can. If it didn't have to do with the theater, Maddy always looked for the easiest way.

When she reached her apartment building, the Gianellis were arguing in their first-floor apartment. Italian expletives streamed up the stairwell. Maddy remembered her mail, jogged back down half a flight and searched her key ring for the tiny, tarnished key that opened the scarred slot. With a postcard from her parents, an offer for life insurance and two bills in hand, she jogged back up again.

On the second landing the newlywed from 242 sat reading a textbook.

"How's the English Lit?" Maddy asked her.

"Pretty good. I think I'll have my certificate by August."

"Terrific." But she looked lonely, Maddy thought, and she paused a moment. "How's Tony?"

"He made the finals for that play off-Broadway." When she smiled, her young, hopeful face glowed. "If he makes chorus he can quit waiting tables at night. He says prosperity's just around the corner."

"That's great, Angie." She didn't add that prosperity was always around the corner for gypsies. The roads just kept getting longer. "I've got to run. Somebody's coming for dinner."

On the third floor she heard the wailing echo of rock music and the thumping of feet. The disco queen was rehearsing, Maddy decided as she chugged up the next flight of steps. After a quick search for her keys, she let herself in. She had an hour.

She switched on the stereo on her way to the kitchen, then dropped her bag on the twelve-inch square of Formica she called counter space. She scrubbed two potatoes, stuck them in the oven, remembered to turn it on, then dumped the fresh vegetables into the sink.

It occurred to her vaguely that she might tidy the place up a bit. It hadn't been dusted in . . . well, there was enough clutter on the tables to hide the dust, anyway. Some might call her rooms a shade messy, but no one would call them dull.

Most of her furnishings and decorations were Broadway surplus. When a show closed—especially if it had flopped—the markdown on props and materials was wonderful. They were memories to her, so even after the money had started to come in regularly she hadn't replaced them. The curtains were red and dizzily ornate—a steal from *Best Little Whorehouse in Texas*. The sofa, with its curvy back and dangerously hard cushions, had been part of the refuse of a flop she couldn't even remember, but it was reputed to have once sat on the parlor set of *My Fair Lady*. Maddy had decided to believe it.

None of the tables matched; nor did any of the chairs. It was a hodgepodge of periods and colors, a tangle of junk and splendor that suited her very well.

Posters lined the walls, posters from plays she'd been in, posters from plays where she hadn't gotten past the first call. There was one plant, a philodendron that hovered between life and death in its vivid pot by the window. It was the last in a long line of dead soldiers.

But her most prized possession was a hot-pink neon sign whose curvy letters spelled out her name. Trace had sent it to her when she'd gotten her first job in a Broadway chorus. Her name in lights. Maddy switched it on as she usually did and thought that while her brother might not often be around, he always made himself known.

Deciding not to spend too much time picking up when it would only be cluttered again in a couple of days, Maddy cleaned off a couple of chairs, stacked the magazines and the unopened mail and left it at that. More pressing was the task of washing out her dance clothes.

She filled the tub with warm water and soap, then added the tights and leotard she'd worn to class that morning. With them she added her rehearsal clothes.

For good measure she dropped in sweatbands and leg warmers. With the sleeves of her knee-length sweat-shirt rolled up, she began the monotonous job of washing out, rinsing and wringing. Using the make-shift clothesline she'd fashioned in the tub, Maddy hung every piece up to dry.

The bathroom was no larger than a closet. When she stood up and turned, she faced herself in the mir-ror over the sink. Mirrors were an intimate part of her life. There were days when she danced in front of them for eight hours, watching, recording, assessing every muscle and move of her body.

Now she looked at her face—fairly good bones, satisfactory features. It was the combination of pointed chin, wide eyes and glowing skin that won those awful accolades like 'cute' and 'wholesome.' Nothing earth-shattering, she thought, but she could give them a hand.

On a whim she swung the mirrored door open and grabbed two handfuls of makeup at random. She bought it, stored it, even hoarded it. It was almost an obsession. The fact that she rarely used it unless she was performing didn't make her hobby seem odd to her. Whenever she wanted to play with her face, she had all the tools handy.

For ten minutes she experimented, putting on, creaming off, then putting on again, until the result was simply a bit of exotic color on her eyes and the faintest hint of warmth on her cheekbones. Maddy put the pots and tubes and pencils back into the cabinet, then shut the door before anything could fall out.

Was she supposed to chill that wine? she thought abruptly. Or maybe she should serve it at room tem-

perature—which was now hovering around eighty degrees.

She must have given him the wrong address. Reed
didn't doubt his memory. He'd been taught early the
importance of remembering names, faces, facts, figures. When your teacher was your father and you
adored your father, you learned. From years of practice rather than from natural inclination, Reed could
hold three columns of figures in his head and tally
each of them. Edwin Valentine had taught his son that
a smart businessman hired the best accountants, then
made certain he knew as much as they did.

He hadn't forgotten the address or mixed up the
numbers, but he was beginning to believe she had.

The neighborhood was tough and seedy and rap-
idly getting seedier as he drove. A broken chair, with
its stuffing pouring out the side, sat on the sidewalk.
A group of people was arguing over ownership. An old
man in an undershirt and shorts sat on a grimy stoop
and chugged a can of beer. He eyed Reed's car owl-
ishly as it passed.

How could she live here? Or more to the point, he
thought, why would she live here? Maddy O'Hurley
had just come off a year's engagement in a solid show
that had brought her a Tony nomination. Before that,
she'd had another year as the second lead and under-
study to the star in a successful revival of *Kiss Me,
Kate.*

Reed knew, because he'd made it his business to
know. His business, he assured himself as he pulled to
the curb in front of the building that corresponded
with the numbers Maddy had given him. A woman
who was about to embark on her third major Broad-

way show could afford to live in a neighborhood
where they didn't mine the sidewalks at night.

As Reed stepped out of his car he spotted a young
hood leaning against a lamppost, eyeing his hubcaps.
With a quiet oath, Reed approached him. He'd
dressed casually, but even without tie and jacket he
looked as if he belonged at the country club.

"How much to watch it?" Reed began bluntly.
"Instead of strip it?"

The boy shifted his position and smiled with prac-
ticed arrogance. "Pretty elegant wheels you got there,
Lancelot. Don't see many BMWs cruise through here.
I'm thinking of getting my camera."

"Take all the pictures you want. Just don't take
anything else." Reed slipped a twenty out of his wallet. "Let's say you're gainfully employed. There's another ten if the car's intact when I come out. You
won't get more by hocking the hubcaps, and this way
all you have to do is take in the evening air."

The boy studied the car, then its driver. He knew
how to size up an opponent and figure the odds. The
flinty eyes were direct and calm. If he'd seen fear in
them, the boy would have pushed. Instead, he took the
twenty.

"You're the boss. I got a couple hours to kill." He
grinned and showed a painfully crooked front tooth.
The twenty had already disappeared before Reed
started toward the front door.

Her name was on a mail-slot in what might loosely
have been called a foyer. Apartment 405. And there
was no elevator. Reed started up the steps to the ac-
companiment of squalling kids, ear-splitting jazz and
the swearing Gianellis. By the time he reached the
third floor, he was doing some swearing himself.

When the knock came, Maddy was up to her wrists in salad. She'd known that he'd be on time just as surely as she'd known she wouldn't be. "Hang on a minute," she shouted, then looked around fruitlessly for a cloth to dry her hands with. Giving up, she shook what moisture she could from them as she walked to the door. She gave the knob a hard yank, then grinned at him.

"Hi. I hope you're not hungry. I'm not finished yet."

"No. I—" He glanced back over his shoulder. "The hall..." he began, and let his words trail off. Maddy stuck her head out and sniffed.

"Smells like a cow pasture," she said. "Guido must be cooking again. Come on in."

He should have been prepared for her apartment, but he wasn't. Reed glanced around at the vivid red curtains, the shock of blue rug, the chair that looked as though it had come straight out of a medieval castle. It had, in fact, come from the set of *Camelot*. Her name in pink neon glowed brilliantly against a white wall.

"Quite a place," he murmured.

"I like it when I'm here." Overhead came three simultaneous thuds. "Ballet student on the fifth," Maddy said easily. "*Tours jeté*. Would you like some wine?"

"Yes." Reed glanced uneasily at the ceiling again. "I think I would."

"Good. So would I." She walked back to the kitchen, which was separated from the living room by a teetering breakfront and imagination. "There's a corkscrew in one of these drawers," she told him. "Why don't you open the bottle while I finish this?"

After a moment's hesitation, Reed found himself searching through Maddy's kitchen drawers. In the first one he found a tennis ball, several loose keys and some snapshots, but no corkscrew. He rifled through another, wondering what he was doing there. On the fifth floor, the ballet student continued his leaps.

"How do you like your steak?"

Reed rescued the corkscrew from a tangle of black wire. "Ahh... medium rare."

"Okay." When she bent down to pull the broiling pan out of a cupboard, her cheek nearly brushed his knee. Reed drew the cork from the bottle, then set the wine aside to let it breathe.

"Why did you ask me to dinner?"

Still bent over and rummaging, Maddy turned her face upward. "No concrete reason. I rarely have one, but if you'd like, why don't we say because of the hairbrush?" She rose then, holding a dented broiling pan. "Besides, you're terrific to look at."

She saw the humor come and go in his eyes and was delighted.

"Thank you."

"Oh, you're welcome." She brushed away the hair that fell into her eyes and thought vaguely that it was about time for a trim. "Why did you come?"

"I don't have any idea."

"That should definitely make things more interesting. You've never backed a play before, have you?"

"No."

"I've never cooked dinner for a backer. So we're even." Setting the salad aside, she began to prepare the steak.

"Glasses?"

"Glasses?" she repeated, then glanced at the wine. "Oh, they're up in one of the cupboards."

Resigned, Reed began another search. He found cups with broken handles, a mismatched set of fabulous bone china and several plastic dishes. Eventually he found a hoard of eight wineglasses, no two alike. "You don't believe in uniformity?"

"Not really." Maddy set the steak under the broiler, then slammed the oven door. "It needs a boost to get going," she told him as she accepted the glass he offered. "To SRO."

"To what?"

"Standing room only." She clicked her glass to his and drank.

Reed studied her over the rim of his glass. She still wore the oversize sweatshirt. Her feet were bare. The scent that hung around her was light, airy and guileless. "You aren't what I expected."

"That's nice. What did you expect?"

"Someone with a sharper edge, I suppose. A little jaded, a little hungry."

"Dancers are always hungry," she said with a half smile, turning to grate cheese onto potatoes.

"I decided you'd asked me here for one of two reasons. The first was to pump me for information about the finances of the play."

Maddy chuckled, putting a sliver of cheese on her tongue. "Reed, I have to worry about eight dance routines—maybe ten, if Macke has his way—six songs, and lines I haven't even counted yet. I'll leave the money matters to you and the producers. What was the second reason?"

"To come on to me."

Her brows lifted, more in curiosity than shock. Reed watched her steadily, his eyes dark and calm, his smile cool and faintly amused. A cynic, Maddy realized, thinking it was a shame. Perhaps he had a reason to be. That was more of a shame. "Do women usually come on to you?"

He'd expected her to be embarrassed, to be annoyed, at the very least to laugh. Instead, she looked at him with mild curiosity. "Let's just pass over that one, shall we?"

"I suppose they do." She began to hunt for a kitchen fork to turn the steak with. "And I suppose you'd resent it after a while. I never had to deal with that sort of thing myself. Men always came on to my sister." She found the fork, squeaked open the oven door and flipped the steak over.

"There's only one," Reed pointed out.

"No, I've got two sisters."

"Steak. You're only cooking one steak."

"Yes, I know. It's yours."

"Aren't you eating?"

"Oh, sure, but I never eat a lot of red meat." She slammed the oven door again. "It clogs up the system. I figured you'd give me a couple bites of yours. Here." She handed him the salad bowl. "Take this over to the little table by the window. We're nearly ready."

It was good. In fact, it was excellent. As he'd watched her haphazard way of cooking, Reed had had his doubts. The salad was a symphony of mixed greens in a spicy vinaigrette. Cheese and bacon were heaped on steaming potatoes, and the steak was done precisely as he preferred. The wine had a subtle bite.

Maddy was still nursing her first glass. She ate a fraction of what seemed normal to Reed, and seemed to relish every bite.

"Take some more steak," he offered, but she shook her head. She did, however, take a second small bowl of salad. "It seems to me that anyone who has as physical a job as you do should eat more to compensate."

"Dancers are better off a little underweight. Mostly it's a matter of eating the right things. I really hate that." She grinned, taking a forkful of lettuce and alfalfa sprouts. "Not that I hate the right kind of food, I just love food, period. Once in a while I splurge on thousands of calories. But I always make sure it's a kind of celebration."

"What kind?"

"Well, say it's rained for three days, then the sun comes out. That's good enough for chocolate-chip cookies." She poured herself another half glass of wine and filled his glass before she noticed his blank expression. "Don't you like chocolate-chip cookies?"

"I've never considered them celebrational."

"You've never lived an abnormal life."

"Do you consider your life abnormal?"

"I don't. Thousands would." She propped her elbows on the table and rested her chin in her hands. Food, so often dreamed over, could always be forgotten when the conversation was interesting. "What's your life like?"

The light from the window beside them was dying quickly. What was left of it gleamed darkly in her hair. Her eyes, which had seemed so open, so easy, now glowed like a cat's, tawny, lazy, watchful. The neon was a foolish pink shimmer that curled into her name. "I don't know how to answer that."

"Well, I can probably guess some of it. You have an apartment, probably overlooking the park." She poked into the salad again, still watching him. "Ming vases, Dresden figures, something of the sort. You spend more time at your office than in your home. Conscientious about your work, dedicated to the business. Any responsible second-generation tycoon would be. You date very casually, because you don't have the time or inclination for a relationship. You'd spend more time at the museum if you could manage it, take in a foreign film now and then, and prefer quiet French restaurants."

She wasn't laughing at him, he decided. But she was more amused than impressed. Annoyance crept into his eyes, not because of her description but because she'd read him so easily. "That's very clever."

"I'm sorry," she said with such quick sincerity that his annoyance vanished. "It's a bad habit of mine, sizing people up, categorizing them. I'd be furious with anyone who did it to me." Then she stopped and caught her bottom lip between her teeth. "How close was I?"

It was difficult to resist her frank good humor. "Close enough."

With a laugh, she shook her head back so that her hair flared out then settled. She brought her legs up into the lotus position. "Is it all right to ask why you're backing a play about a stripper?"

"Is it all right to ask why you're starring in a play about a stripper?"

She beamed at him like a teacher, Reed thought, whose student had answered a question with particular insight. "It's a terrific play. The trick to being sure of that is to look at the script without the songs and the dance numbers. The music punctuates, emphasizes, exhilarates, but even without it, it's a good story. I like the way Mary develops without having to change intrinsically. She's had to be tough to survive, but she's made the best of it. She wants more, and she goes after it because she deserves more. The only glitch is that she really falls for this guy. He's everything she's ever wanted in a material way, but she really just plain loses her head over him. After she does, the money doesn't matter, the position doesn't matter, but she ends up with it all anyway. I like that."

"Happy ever after?"

"Don't you believe in happy endings?"

A shutter clicked down over his expression, quickly, completely. Curiously. "In a play."

"I should tell you about my sister."

"The one the men came on to?"

"No, my other sister. Would you like an éclair? I bought you one, and if you have it you could offer me a bite. It would be rude for me to refuse."

Damn it, she was getting more appealing by the minute. Not his type, not his speed, not his style. But he smiled at her. "I'd love an éclair."

Maddy went into the kitchen, rummaged noisily, then came back with a fat chocolate-iced pastry. "My sister Abby," she began, "married Chuck Rockwell, the race driver. Do you know about him?"

"Yes." Reed had never been an avid fan of auto racing, but the name rang a bell. "He was killed a few years back."

"Their marriage hadn't been working. Abby really had been having a dreadful time. She was raising her two children alone on this farm in Virginia. Financially she was strapped, emotionally she was drained. A few months ago she authorized a biography of Rockwell. The writer came to the farm, ready, I think, to gun Abby down,'' Maddy continued, placing the éclair on the table. ''Are you going to offer me a bite?''

Reed obligingly cut a piece of the pastry with his fork and offered it to her. Maddy let the crust and cream and icing lie on her tongue for a long, decadent moment. ''So what happened to your sister?''

''She married the writer six weeks ago.'' When she smiled again, her face simply lighted up, just as emphatically as the pink neon. ''Happy-ever-after doesn't just happen in plays.''

''What makes you think your sister's second marriage will work?''

''Because this is the right one.'' She leaned forward again, her eyes on his. ''My sisters and I are triplets, we know each other inside out. When Abby married Chuck, I was sorry. In my heart, you see, I knew it wasn't right, that it could never be right, because I know Abby just as well as I know myself. I could only hope it would work somehow. When she married Dylan, it was such a different feeling—like letting out a long breath and relaxing.''

''Dylan Crosby?''

''Yes, do you know him?''

''He did a book on Richard Bailey. Richard's been signed with Valentine Records for twenty years. I got to know Dylan fairly well when he was doing his research.''

''Small world.''

"Yes." It was full dusk now, and the sky was deepening to purple, but she didn't bother with lights. The ballet student had long since stopped his practicing. Somewhere down the hall, a baby could be heard wailing fitfully. "Why do you live here?"

"Here?" She gave him a blank look. "Why not?"

"You've got Attila the Hun on the street corner, screaming neighbors . . ."

"And?" she added, prompting him.

"You could move uptown."

"What for? I know this neighborhood. I've been here for seven years. It's close to Broadway, handy to rehearsal halls and classes. Probably half the tenants in this building are gypsies."

"I wouldn't be surprised."

"No, chorus-line gypsies." She laughed and began to toy with the leaf of the philodendron. It was a nervous gesture she wouldn't have begun to recognize herself. "Dancers who move from show to show, hoping for that one big break. I got it. That doesn't mean I'm not still a gypsy." She glanced back at him, wondering why it should matter so much that he understand her. "You can't change what you are, Reed. Or at least you shouldn't."

He believed that, and always had. He was the son of Edwin Valentine, one of the early movers and shakers in the record industry. He was a product of success, wealth and survival. He was, as Maddy had said, devoted to the business, because it had been part of his life always. He was impatient, often ruthless, a man who looked at the bottom line and the fine print before changing it to suit himself. He had no business sitting in a darkening apartment with a woman with cat's eyes and a wicked smile. He had less business entertaining fantasies about what it would be like to remain until the moon began to rise.

"You're killing that plant," he murmured.

"I know. I always do." She had to swallow, and that surprised her. Something in the way he'd been looking at her just now. Something in the tone of his voice, the set of his body. She could always be mistaken about a face, but not about a body. His was tensed, and so was hers. "I keep buying them, and keep killing them."

"Too much sun." He hadn't meant to, but brushed the back of her hand with his fingers. "And too much water. It's as easy to overlove as underlove."

"I hadn't thought of that." She was thinking about the tremors that were shooting up her arm, down her spine. "Your plants probably thrive with the perfect balance of attention." She caught herself wondering if it was the same with his women. Then she rose, because her system wasn't reacting as she'd expected it to. "I can offer you tea, but not coffee. I don't have any."

"No. I have to go." He didn't—there were no schedules to be met, no appointments to keep. But he was a survivor, and he knew when to back away. "I enjoyed the dinner, Maddy. And the company."

She let out a long breath, as if she'd just come down from a very high leap. "I'm glad. We'll do it again."

It was impulse. It was usually impulse with Maddy. She didn't think about it twice. With friendly warmth, she put her hands on his shoulders and touched her lips to his. The kiss lasted less than a second. And vibrated like a hurricane.

He felt her lips, smooth, curved a bit in a smile. He tasted the sweetness, fleeting, with a touch of spice.

Her scent was there, hovering, light enough to tease. When she moved back, he heard her quick, surprised intake of air and saw the same surprise reflected in her eyes.

What was that? she thought. What in God's name was that? She was a woman who made a habit of light, friendly kisses, quick hugs, casual touches. None of them had ever rocked her like this. She felt hints of everything she'd ever imagined in that one brief contact. And she wanted more. Because she'd practiced self-denial all her life, it was easier to control the desire to touch the fire a second time.

"I'm glad you came." The tremor in her voice amazed her.

"So am I." It wasn't often he had to use restraint. It wasn't often he had to deny himself anything. In this case, he knew he had to. "Good night, Maddy."

"Good night." She stood where she was while he let himself out. Then, listening to her body, she sat down. Better to think this one through, she warned herself. Better to think long and hard. Then her gaze drifted over to the plant that was wilting and yellowing in the dark window. Strange, she hadn't realized she'd been in the dark herself for so long.

Chapter Three

Her muscles warmed, her eyes dreamy, Maddy stretched at the *barre* with the line of dancers. The instructor called out every position, *plié*, *tendu*, *attitude*. Legs, torsos, arms responded in endless repetition.

Morning class was repetition, a continual reminder to the body that it could indeed do the unnatural and do it well time and time again. Without it, that same body would simply revolt and refuse to strain itself, refuse to turn the leg out from the hip as though it were on a ball hinge, refuse to bend beyond what was ordinary, refuse to stretch itself past natural goals. It would, in essence, become normal.

It wasn't necessary to concentrate fully. Maddy's body had built-in discipline, built-in instinct that carried her through the warm-up. Her mind floated away, far enough to dream, close enough to hear the calls.

Grand plié. Her knees bent, her body descended slowly until her crotch hovered over her heels. Muscles trembled, then acquiesced. She wondered if Reed was already in his office, though it was still shy of nine. She thought he would be. She imagined he would arrive as a matter of habit before his secretary, before his assistant. Would he think of her at all?

Attitude en avant. Her leg raised, holding at a ninety-degree angle. She continued to hold as the count dragged on. He probably wouldn't, Maddy concluded. His mind was so crowded with schedules and appointments that he wouldn't have time for a single wayward thought.

Battement fondu. She brought her foot under her supporting knee, which bent in synchronization. Gradually, slowly, she straightened, feeling the resistance, using it. He didn't have to think of her now. Later, perhaps, on his way home, over a quiet drink, his mind might drift to her. She wanted to think so.

Maddy's serviceable gray leotard was damp when she moved onto the floor for center practice. The exercises they had just practiced at the *barre* would be repeated again. On signal, she went into the fifth position and began.

One, two, three, four. Two, two, three, four.

It was raining outside. Maddy could watch the water stream down the small frosted windows as she bent, stretched, reached and held on command. A warm rain, she thought. The air had been steamy and heavy when she'd rushed to class that morning. She hoped it wouldn't stop before she got out again.

There hadn't been much time for walking in the rain when she'd been a child. Not that she regretted anything. Still, she and her family had spent more time at rehearsals and in train stations than in parks and playgrounds. Her parents had brought the fun with them—games, riddles and stories. Such high-flown, ridiculous stories, stories that were worlds in themselves. When you were blessed with two Irish parents who possessed fantastic imaginations, the sky was the limit.

She'd learned so much from them—more than timing, more than projection. Little formal education had seeped through, but geography had been taught on the road. Seeing the Mississippi had been more illuminating than reading about it. English, grammar, literature had come through the books that her parents had loved and passed on. Practical math had been a matter of survival. Her education had been as unconventional as her recreation, but she considered herself more well-rounded than most.

Maddy hadn't missed the parks or playgrounds. Her childhood had been its own carousel. But now, as a woman, she rarely missed a chance to walk in a warm summer rain.

Walking in the rain wouldn't appeal to Reed. In fact, Maddy doubted it would even occur to him. They were worlds apart—by birth, by choice, by inclination. Her right foot slid into a *chassé*, back, forward, to the side. Repeat. Repeat. He would be logical, sensible, perhaps a bit ruthless. You couldn't succeed in business otherwise. No one would consider it logical to stretch your body into unnatural positions day after day. No one would consider it sensible to throw yourself body and soul into the theater and subject yourself to the whims of the public. If she was ruthless, she was only ruthless in the demands she made on herself physically.

So why couldn't she stop thinking about him? She couldn't stop wondering. She couldn't stop remembering the way the dying sunlight had lingered on his hair, darkening it, deepening it—or the way his eyes had stayed on hers, direct, intrigued and cynical. Was it foolish for an optimist to be attracted to a cynic? Of course it was. But she'd done more foolish things.

They'd shared one kiss, and barely a kiss at that. His arms hadn't come around her. His lips hadn't pressed hungrily to hers. Yet she'd relived that instant of contact again and again. Somehow she thought—somehow she was sure—he hadn't been unmoved. However foolish it was, she dredged up that quick flood of sensation and reexperienced it. It added a fine sheen of heat to already-warmed skin. Her heartbeat, already thudding rhythmically with the demands of the exercise, increased in speed.

Amazing, she thought, that the memory of a sensation could do so much. Launching into a series of *pirouettes*, Maddy brought the feeling back again and spun with it.

With her hair still dripping from the shower, Maddy pulled on a pair of patched bright yellow bib overalls. The rehearsal hall showers themselves were ripe with the scents of splash-on cologne and powdered talc. A tall woman, naked to the waist, sat in the corner and worked a cramp out of her calf.

"I really appreciate you telling me about this class." Wanda, resplendent in jeans and a sweater as snug as skin, tugged her own hair back into a semiorganized bun. "It's tougher than the one I was taking. And five dollars cheaper."

"Madame has a soft spot for gypsies." Maddy straddled a long bench, bent over and began to aim a hand drier at the underside of her hair.

"Not everyone in your position is willing to share."

"Come on, Wanda."

"It isn't all a big sisterhood, sweetheart." Wanda jammed in a last pin and watched Maddy's reflection in the mirror. Even with the reddish hair curtaining her face, Wanda saw the faint frown of disagreement. "You're the lead, and you can't tell me you don't feel newcomers breathing down your neck."

"Makes you work harder." Maddy shook back her hair, too impatient to dry it. "Where'd you get those earrings?"

Wanda finished fastening on the fiercely red prisms, which fell nearly to her shoulders. A movement of her head sent them spinning. Both she and Maddy silently approved the result. "A boutique in the Village. Five-seventy-one."

Maddy got up from the bench and stood with her head close to Wanda's. She narrowed her eyes and imagined. "Did they have them in blue?"

"Probably. You like gaudy?"

"I love gaudy."

"Trade you these for that sweatshirt you've got with the eyes all over it."

"Deal," Maddy said immediately. "I'll bring it to rehearsal."

"You look happy."

Maddy smiled and rose on her toes to bring her ear closer to Wanda's. "I am happy."

"I mean, you look *man* happy."

With a lift of her brow, Maddy studied her own face in the mirror. Free of makeup, her skin glowed with health. Her mouth was full and shaped well enough to do without paint. It was a pity, she'd always thought, that her lashes were rather light and stubby. Chantel had gotten darker, longer ones.

"Man happy," Maddy repeated, enjoying the phrase. "I did meet a man."

"Shows. Good-looking?"

"Wonderful-looking. He's got incredible gray eyes. Really gray, no green at all. And a kind of cleft." She touched her own chin.

"Let's talk body."

Maddy let out a peal of laughter and hooked her arm around Wanda's shoulders. Friendships, the best of them, are often made quickly, she thought. "Good shoulders, very trim. He holds himself well. I'd guess good muscle tone."

"Guess?"

"I haven't seen him naked."

"Well, honey, what's your problem?"

"We only had dinner." Maddy was used to frank sexual talk. A lot more used to the talk than to acting on it. "I think he was interested—in sort of a detached way."

"So you've got to make him interested in an attached way. He's not a dancer, is he?"

"No."

"Good." Wanda sent her earrings for a last spin, then began to unfasten them. "Dancers make lousy husbands. I know."

"Well, I'm not thinking of marrying him..." she began, then widened her eyes. "Were you married to a dancer?"

"Five years ago. We were in the chorus of *Pippin*. Ended up getting married on opening night." She handed the earrings over. "Trouble was, before the play closed he'd forgotten that the ring on my finger applied to him."

"I'm sorry Wanda."

"It was a lesson," she said with a shrug. "Don't jump into something legal with a smooth-talking, good-looking man. Unless he's loaded," she added. "Is yours?"

"Is my— Oh." Maddy pouted into the mirror. "I suppose."

"Then grab ahold. If it doesn't work out, you can dry your eyes with a nice fat settlement."

"I don't think you're as cynical as you'd like to appear." Maddy gave Wanda's shoulder a quick squeeze. "Hurt bad?"

"It stung." Wanda found it odd that she'd never admitted that to anyone but herself before. "Let's just say I learned that marriage doesn't work unless two people play by the rules. How about some breakfast?"

"No, I can't." She glanced down to where her drooping philodendron sat under the bench. "I've got to deliver something."

"That." Wanda broke into a grin. "Looks like it needs a decent burial."

"It needs," Maddy corrected as she fastened on her new earrings, "the proper balance of attention."

He hadn't stopped thinking about her. Reed wasn't used to anything interfering with his schedule—especially not a flighty, eccentric woman with neon on her walls. They didn't have a thing in common. He'd told himself that repeatedly the night before, when he hadn't been able to sleep. She had nothing to attract him. Unless you counted whiskey-colored eyes. Or a laugh that came out of nowhere, and that could echo in your mind for hours.

He preferred women with classic tastes, elegant manners. The companions he chose wouldn't drive through Maddy's neighborhood with an armed guard, much less live there. They certainly wouldn't nibble at the meat on his plate. The women he dated went to the theater. They didn't act in it. They certainly wouldn't allow a man to see them sweat.

Why, after a few very brief encounters with Maddy O'Hurley, was Reed beginning to think the women he'd dated were raging bores? Of course they weren't. Reed began to study the sales figures in front of him again. He'd never dated a woman merely for her looks. He wanted and sought intelligent conversation, mutual interests, humor, style. He might want to discuss the impressionist show at the Metropolitan over dinner or the weather conditions in St. Moritz over brandy.

What he avoided—studiously avoided—was any woman connected with the entertainment field. He respected entertainers, admired them, but kept them at arm's length on a social level. As head of Valentine Records he dealt constantly with singers, musicians, agents, representatives. Valentine Records wasn't just a business. Not as his father had seen it. It was an organization that provided the best in music, from Bach to rock, and prized the talent it had signed and developed.

Reed had entertained musicians from childhood. He considered himself understanding of their needs, their ambitions, their vulnerabilities. In his free time he preferred the company of the less complicated. The less driven. His own ambitions were intense enough. Valentine Records was at the top of the heap and would remain there. He would see to that. Not only for his father, but for himself. If, as it often happened, he had to work ten hours a day for and with entertainers, he needed a breather from them when the day was over.

But he couldn't stop thinking of Maddy.

What made her tick? Reed pushed aside the sales figures and turned to look at his view of midtown. The rain turned it all into a misty gray fantasy. She didn't appear to have developed the protective shield that her profession seemed to require. She was rising to the top, like cream, but didn't seem awed by it. Could she really be as basic and uncomplicated as she seemed?

Why did he care?

He'd eaten dinner with her—one short, simple dinner. They'd had an interesting, somewhat intimate conversation. They'd shared a brief, friendly kiss. That had rocked him back on his heels.

So he was attracted. He wasn't immune to bright, vital looks or a firm, compact body. It was natural to be curious about the woman, with her odd philosophies and dangling thought patterns. If he wanted to see her again, there was no harm in it. And it was simple enough. He'd just pick up the phone and call her. They could have dinner again...on his terms. Before the evening was over, he'd discover what it was about her that nagged at him.

When his door opened, Reed's glance of annoyance turned into a warm smile few were ever treated to. "A little wet for golf?"

"Club's a tomb when it rains." Edwin Valentine walked into the room with the long, slow steps of a big man, then dropped heavily into a chair. "Besides, I start to feel old if I don't make it in here every couple of weeks."

"Yeah, you look feeble." Reed leaned back in his chair and studied his father's ruddy, strong-featured face. "What's your handicap these days?"

"Four." Edwin grinned, pleased as a boy. "All in the wrist. Got wind you've all but signed Libby Barlow away from Galloway Records."

Cautious, always cautious, Reed merely inclined his head. "It looks that way."

Edwin nodded. The office had been his for nearly twenty years. The decisions had been his then. Still, he didn't feel any twinge of regret, any twist of envy at seeing his son behind the desk. That was what he'd worked for. "Great set of pipes on that little lady. I'd like to see Dorsey produce her first album with us."

Reed's lips curved slightly. His father's instincts were, as always, bull's-eye. "It's been discussed. I still think you should have an office here." He held up a hand before his father could speak. "I don't mean you should tie yourself down to regular hours again."

"Never had regular hours in my life," Edwin put in.

"Well, irregular hours, then. I do think Valentine Records should have Edwin Valentine."

"It has you." Edwin folded his hands, and the look he gave his son was direct and calm. More, much more passed between them than the words. "Not that I don't think you could use some advice from the old man now and again. However, you're at the helm now. The ship's holding steady."

"I wouldn't let you down."

Edwin recognized the intensity in his son's voice, and understood a portion of the passion behind it.

"I'm aware of that, Reed. I don't have to tell you that of all the things that have touched my life, nothing's made me prouder than you."

Emotion rippled through him. Gratitude, love. "Dad—"

Before he could finish, or even properly begin, his secretary wheeled in a tray of coffee and sweet rolls. "By damn, Hannah, you're as sharp as ever."

"So are you, Mr. Valentine. Looks like you've dropped a pound or two." She fixed his coffee the way he preferred it. The flash of a wink she sent Reed was too quick to measure. She'd been with the company twelve years and was the only person on staff who would have dared the cheeky look.

"You witch, Hannah. I've gained five." Edwin heaped two rolls on his plate anyway.

"You wear it well, Mr. Valentine. You have a meeting at eleven-thirty with Mackenzie in Sales." She set another cup on Reed's desk. "Would you like for me to reschedule?"

"Not on my account," Edwin put in quickly.

Reed glanced at his watch and calculated the next thirty-five minutes. "I'll see him at eleven-thirty, Hannah. Thank you."

"Hell of a woman," Edwin said with a full mouth as the door shut behind Hannah. "Smart move, taking her on as your secretary when I retired."

"I don't think Valentine Records could run without Hannah." Reed glanced at the rain-drenched window again, thinking of another woman.

"What's on your mind, Reed?"

"Hmm?" Bringing himself back to the conversation, Reed picked up his coffee. "The sales figures look good. I think you'll be pleased with the results at the end of the fiscal year.''

Edwin didn't doubt that. Reed was a product of his mind, of his heart. Only rarely did it concern him that he'd molded his son a little too closely after himself. ''Doesn't look to me like you've got sales figures on the brain.''

Reed nodded, deciding to answer the question while evading it. ''I've been giving a lot of thought to the play we're backing.''

Edwin smiled a little. ''Still nervous about my hunch there?''

''No.'' He could answer that honestly enough now. ''I've had several meetings with the producer and the director. I've even looked in on a couple of rehearsals. My guess is that the play itself will hit big. The score—more our concern, really—is wonderful. What we're working on now is promotion and marketing for the cast album.''

''If you wouldn't mind, I might like to squirrel my way in on that end a bit.''

''You know you don't have to ask.''

''I do,'' Edwin corrected. ''You're in charge, Reed. I didn't step down figuratively, but literally. As it happens, though, this is a pet project of mine. I've got a bit of personal interest.''

''You've never explained why you do.''

Edwin smiled a bit and broke off a corner of his second roll. ''Goes back awhile. A long while. Have you met Maddy O'Hurley yet?''

Reed's brows drew together. Did his father read him that well? ''As a matter of fact—'' When the buzzer sounded on his desk, he accepted the interruption without heat. ''Yes, Hannah.''

"I'm sorry to disturb you, Mr. Valentine, but there's a young woman out here." Hannah could be tough as nails, but she found herself smiling at the drenched figure in front of her. "She says she has something to deliver to you."

"Take it, will you, Hannah?"

"She prefers to give it to you personally. Her name is, ah . . . Maddy."

Reed paused on the brink of refusal. "Maddy? Send her in, Hannah."

Dripping rain and carrying her dance bag and her dying plant, Maddy rushed into the office. "I'm sorry to bother you, Reed. It's just that I've been thinking and I decided you should have this before I murder it. I always get these spasms of guilt when I kill another plant and I figured you could spare me."

Edwin rose as she passed his chair, and she broke off her tumbling explanation. "Hello." She sent him an easy smile and tried to ignore the sweet rolls on the tray. "I'm interrupting, but it's really a matter of life and death." She set the wet, wilting plant on his spotless oak desk. "Don't tell me if it dies, okay? But if it survives, you let me know. Thanks." With a last flashing grin, she started to leave.

"Maddy." Now that she'd given him a moment to speak, Reed rose, as well. "I'd like you to meet my father. Edwin Valentine, Maddy O'Hurley."

"Oh." Maddy started to offer her hand, then dropped it again. "I'm soaked," she explained, smiling instead. "It's nice to meet you."

"Delighted." Edwin beamed at her. "Have a seat."

"Oh, I can't, really. I'm wet."

"A little water never hurt good leather." Before she could protest, Edwin took her arm and led her to one of the wide, biscuit-colored chairs beside the desk. "I've admired you onstage."

"Thank you." It didn't occur to her to be awed, though she was sitting almost toe-to-toe with one of the richest and most influential men in the country. She found his wide, ruddy face appealing, and though she looked, she couldn't find a single resemblance to his son.

Reed brought her gaze back to his. "Would you like some coffee, Maddy?"

No, he didn't resemble his father. Reed was sharp-featured and lean. Hungry. Maddy found her blood moving just a bit faster. "I don't drink coffee anymore. If you had any tea with honey, I'd love a cup."

"Have a roll," Edwin said when he saw her give them a quick, wistful look.

"I'm going to miss lunch," she told him easily. "I guess I could use a little sugar in the bloodstream." She smiled at him as she chose one that dripped with frosting. If she was going to sin, she preferred to sin well. "We've all been wondering if you'd come by rehearsals, Mr. Valentine."

"I've given it some thought. Reed and I were just talking about the play. He's of the opinion it's going to be a hit. What do you think?"

"I think it's bad luck for me to say so until we try it out in Philadelphia." She took a bite of the roll and could almost feel her energy level rise. "I can say that the dance numbers should knock them back in the aisles." She looked gratefully at Hannah as the secretary brought in her tea. "We're working on one this afternoon that should bring down the house. If it doesn't, I'll have to go back to waiting tables."

"I trust your judgment." Edwin reached over to pat her hand. "To my way of thinking, if an O'Hurley doesn't know when a dance number works, no one does." At her puzzled smile, he leaned back. "I knew your parents."

"You did?" Her face lighted with pleasure, the roll forgotten. "I don't remember either of them talking about it."

"A long time ago." He sent Reed a quick glance as if in explanation, and continued. "I was just getting started, hustling talent, hustling money. I met your parents right here in New York. I was on the down end right then, scrambling for pennies and backers. They let me sleep on a cot in their hotel room. I've never forgotten."

Maddy sent a meaningful glance around the office. "Well, you scrambled enough pennies, Mr. Valentine."

He laughed, urging more rolls on her. "I always wanted to pay them back, you know. Told them I would. That was a good twenty-five years ago. You and your sisters were still in booties. I do believe I helped your mother change your diaper."

She grinned at him. "It was very difficult to tell Chantel, Abby and me apart, even from that angle."

"You had a brother," he remembered. "A pistol."

"He still is."

"Sang like an angel. I told your father I'd sign him up once I got myself going. By the time I did and managed to find your family again, your brother was gone."

"To Pop's continued lamentations, Trace decided against a life on the road. Or at least he opted to follow a different road."

"You and your sisters had a group."

Maddy was never sure whether to wince or laugh at the memory. "The O'Hurley Triplets."

"I was going to offer you a contract," he said, and watched her eyes widen. "Absolutely. About that time, your sister Abby got married."

A record contract? More, a contract with Valentine Records! Maddy thought back to those times and imagined the awe that would have accompanied such an announcement. "Did Pop know?"

"We'd talked."

"Lord." She shook her head. "It must have killed him to see that slip through his fingers, but he never said a word. Chantel and I finished out the bookings after Abby married, then she went west and I went east. Poor Pop."

"I'd say you've given him plenty to be proud of."

"You're a nice man, Mr. Valentine. Is backing the play a kind of repayment for a night on a cot?"

"A repayment that's going to make my company a lot of money. I'd like to see your parents again, Maddy."

"I'll see what I can do." She rose then, knowing she was pushing her luck if she wanted to get back across town on time to rehearsals. "I didn't mean to take up your visit with your father, Reed."

"Don't apologize." As he stood he continued to watch her, as he had been for the entire visit. "It was enlightening."

She studied him then. He looked so right there, behind the desk, in front of the window, in an office with oil paintings and leather chairs. "We mentioned small worlds once before."

Her hair was dripping down her back. Ridiculous red glass triangles dangled from her ears, looking somehow valiant. The yellow bib overalls and the bright blue T-shirt seemed the only spots of color on a gloomy day. "Yes, we did."

"You'll take the plant, won't you?"

He glanced at it. It was pitiful. "I'll do what I can, but I can't promise a thing."

"Promises make me nervous, anyway. If you take them, you have to make them." She took a deep breath, knowing she should go but not quite able to break away. "Your office is just how I pictured. Organized elegance. It suits you. Thanks for the tea."

He wanted to touch her. It amazed him that he had to fight an urge to walk around the desk and put his hands on her. "Anytime."

"How about Friday?" she blurted out.

"Friday?"

"I'm free on Friday." Now that she'd done it, Maddy decided not to regret it. "I'm free on Friday," she repeated. "After rehearsal. I could meet you."

He nearly shook his head. He had no idea what was on his calendar. He had no idea what to say to a woman who took a casual statement as gospel. He had no idea why he was glad she had. "Where?"

She smiled at him so that every part of her face moved with it. "Rockefeller Center. Seven o'clock. I'm going to be late." She turned and held out her hands to Edwin. "I'm so glad you were here." In her easy way, she leaned down to kiss his cheek. "Goodbye."

"Goodbye, Maddy." Edwin waited until she'd dashed out before turning back to his son. It wasn't often Edwin saw that dazed look on Reed's face. "A man runs into a hurricane like that, he better strap himself down or enjoy the ride." Edwin grinned and took the last roll. "Damned if I wouldn't enjoy the ride."

Chapter Four

Reed wondered if she was playing tricks with his mind. Maddy O'Hurley didn't look like most people's idea of a witch, but that was certainly the most reasonable explanation for the fact that he was loitering around Rockefeller Center at seven on a humid Friday evening. He should have been home by now, enjoying a quiet dinner before diving into the mass of paperwork he carried in his briefcase.

Traffic streamed along Fifth, bad-tempered from heat and noise. Those lucky enough to have a place to go and the time to spare were heading out of town, hoping the heat wave would ease by Monday. Pedestrians hurried by, ties loose, shirts wilting, looking like desert nomads in search of an oasis—an air-conditioned lounge and a long, cold drink.

He watched without interest as a few children, their eyes shrewd enough to mark out-of-towners, tried to push stiff red carnations for a dollar each. They did a fair trade, but not one of them bothered to approach Reed. He looked neither generous nor naive.

Though he caught snippets of conversation as people shuffled past, he didn't bother to wonder about them. He was too busy wondering about himself.

Why had he agreed to meet her? The answer to that was obvious enough. He'd wanted to see her. There was no use picking at that bone again. She aroused his . . . curiosity, Reed decided, unable to find a better term. A woman like her was bound to arouse anyone's curiosity. She was successful, yet she shrugged off the trappings of success. She was attractive, though she rarely played on her looks. Her eyes were honest—if you were the type who trusted such things. Yes, Maddy was a curiosity.

But why in hell hadn't he been able to pull his thoughts together and suggest some place more . . . suitable, at least?

A group of teenage girls streamed past, giggling. Reed sidestepped in lieu of being mowed down. One of them glanced back at him, attracted by the aloof expression and lean body. She put her hand over her mouth and whispered urgently to her companion. There was another round of laughter, and then they were lost in the crowd.

A sidewalk vendor hawked ice-cream bars and did a thriving business with a pack of office workers who hadn't escaped the heat of the city for the weekend. A panhandler milled through the crowd and was far less successful. Reed brushed off a scalper who promised the last two tickets for the evening show down the street at Radio City, then watched him pounce on an elderly pair of tourists. A block away, a siren began to scream. No one even bothered to look.

Reed felt perspiration trickle down his collar and ease down his back. His watch showed 7:20.

His temper was on its last notch when he saw her. Why did she look different, he wondered, from the dozens of people churning around her? Her hair and clothes were bright, but there were others dressed more vividly. She walked with a relaxed sort of grace, but not slowly. It seemed she did nothing slowly. Yet there was an air of ease about her. Reed knew that if he bothered to look he could find five women in that many minutes who had more beauty. But his eyes were fixed on her, and so was his mind.

Sidetracked by the panhandler, Maddy stood near the curb and dug into her purse. She pulled out some change, exchanged what appeared to be a few friendly words, then slid through the crowd. She spotted Reed a moment later and quickened her pace.

"I'm sorry. I'm always apologizing for being late. I missed my bus, but I thought I'd be better off going home and changing after rehearsal because you'd probably be wearing a suit." She looked him over with a bright, satisfied smile. "And I was right."

She'd traded the overalls for a full-skirted dress in a rainbow of colors that made her appear to be the gypsy she claimed she was. Everyone on the sidewalk seemed to fade to gray beside her.

"You might have taken a cab," he murmured, keeping that short but vital distance between them.

"I've never gotten in the habit. I'll spring for dinner and make up for it." She hooked her arm through his with such quick, easy camaraderie that his normal hesitancy toward personal contact never had a chance.

"I bet you're starving after standing around waiting for me. I'm starving, and I didn't." She shifted her body to avoid a collision with a woman in a hurry. "There's a great pizza place just down—"

He cut her off as he drew her through the crowd. "I'll buy. And we can do better than pizza."

Maddy was impressed when he caught a cab on the first try, and she didn't argue when he gave the driver an upscale address off Park Avenue. "I suppose I can switch gears from pizza," she said, always willing to be surprised. "By the way, I like your father."

"I can tell you the feeling was mutual."

Maddy didn't blink when the cab was cut off at a light and the driver began to mutter what might have been curses in what might have been Arabic. "Isn't it odd about him knowing my parents? My pop loves to drop names until they bounce off the walls—especially if he's never met the person. But he never mentioned your father."

Reed wondered if her scent would linger in the stale, steamy air of the cab after they left. He thought somehow it would. "Perhaps he forgot."

Maddy gave a quick, chuckling snort. "Not likely. Once Pop met the niece of the wife of a man whose brother had worked as an extra on *Singin' in the Rain*. He never forgot that. It does seem odd that your father would remember, though, or that it would matter, one night on a cot in a hotel room."

It had seemed unlikely to Reed, as well. Edwin met hundreds and hundreds of people. Why should he remember so clearly a pair of traveling entertainers who had given him a bed one night? "I can only guess that your parents made an impression on him," Reed answered, thinking aloud.

"They are pretty great. So's this," she added as the cab pulled up in front of an elegantly understated French restaurant. "I don't get up this way very often."

"Why?"

"Everything I need's basically concentrated in one area." She would have slid from the cab on the street side if Reed hadn't taken her hand and pulled her out with him onto the curb. "I don't have time to date often, and when I do it's usually with men whose French is limited to ballet positions."

She stopped herself when Reed opened the door for her. "That was a remarkably unchic thing to say, wasn't it?"

They stepped inside, where it was cool, softly scented and quietly pastel. "Yes. But somehow I don't think you worry about being chic."

"I'll figure out whether that was a compliment or an insult later," Maddy decided. "Insults make me cranky, and I don't want to spoil my dinner."

"Ah, Monsieur Valentine."

"Jean-Paul." Reed nodded to the maître d'. "I didn't make a reservation. I hope you have room for us."

"For you, of course." He cast a quick, professional look at Maddy. Not the *monsieur*'s usual type, Jean-Paul decided, but appealing all the same. "Please, follow me."

Maddy followed, wondering what kind of juggling act the maître d' would have to perform. She didn't doubt that Reed would make it worth his while.

It was precisely the sort of restaurant Maddy had thought he would patronize. A bit staid but very elegant, quietly chic without being trendy. Floral pastels on the walls and subdued lighting lent an air of relaxation. The scent of spice was subtle. Maddy took her seat at the corner table and glanced with frank curiosity at the other patrons. So much polish in one small place, she mused. But that was part of the charm of New York. Trash or glitz, you only had to turn a corner.

"Champagne, Mr. Valentine?"

"Maddy?" Reed inclined his head, holding the wine list but leaving the decision to her.

She gave the maître d' a smile that made his opinion of her rise several notches. "It's always difficult to say no to champagne."

"Thank you, Jean-Paul," Reed said, handing back the list after making his selection.

"This is nice." Maddy turned from her study of the other diners to smile at Reed. "I really hadn't expected anything like this."

"What did you expect?"

"That's why I like seeing you. I never know what to expect. I wondered if you'd come by rehearsals again."

He didn't want to admit that he'd wanted to, had had to discipline himself to stay away from something that wasn't his field. "It's not necessary. I have nothing creative to contribute to the play itself. Our concern is the score."

She gave him a solemn look. "I see." Slowly she traced a pattern on the linen cloth. "Valentine Records need the play to be a hit in order to get a return on its investment. And a hit play sells more albums."

"Naturally, but we feel the play's in good hands."

"Well, that should be a comfort to me." But she had to drum up enthusiasm when the champagne arrived. Because rituals amused her, Maddy watched the procedure—the display of the label, the quick, precise opening resulting in a muffled pop, the tasting and approval. The wine was poured in fluted glasses, and she watched the bubbles rise frantically from bottom to top.

"I suppose we should drink to Philadelphia." She was smiling again when she lifted her glass to his.

"Philadelphia?"

"Opening there often tells the tale." She touched her glass to his, then sipped slowly. She would limit her intake of wine just as religiously as she limited her intake of everything else. But she'd enjoy every bit of it. "Wonderful. The last time I had champagne was at a party they threw for me when I left *Suzanna's Park*, but it wasn't nearly this good."

"Why did you?"

"Did I what?"

"Leave the play."

Before she answered, she sipped again. Wine was so pretty in candlelight, she mused. It was a pity people stopped noticing things like that when they could have wine whenever they liked. "I'd given the part everything I could and gotten everything I could out of it." She shrugged. "It was time to move on. I have restless feet, Reed. They dance to the piper."

"You don't look for security?"

"With my background, security doesn't come high on the list. You find it first in yourself, anyway."

He knew about restlessness, about women who moved from one place to the next, never quite finding satisfaction. "Some might say you bored easily."

Something in his tone put her on guard, but she had no way of answering except with honesty. "I'm never bored. How could I be? There's too much to enjoy."

"So you don't consider it a matter of losing interest?"

Without knowing why, she felt he was testing her somehow. Or was he testing himself? "I can't think of anything I've ever lost interest in. No, that's not true. There was this calico-cat pillow, an enormous, expensive one. I thought I was crazy about it, then I bought it and got it home and decided it was awful. But that's not what you mean, is it?"

"No." Reed studied her as he drank. "It's not."

"It's more a matter of different outlooks." She ran a finger around the rim of her glass. "A man like you structures his own routine, then has to live up to it every day because dozens of people are depending on you. A great deal of my life is structured for me, simply to keep me on level ground. The rest has to change, fluctuate constantly, or I lose the edge. You should understand that, you work with entertainers."

His lips curved as he lifted his glass. "I certainly do."

"They amuse you?"

"In some ways," he admitted easily enough. "In others they frustrate me, but that doesn't mean I don't admire them."

"While knowing they're all a little mad."

It took only an instant for the humor to spread from his mouth to his eyes. "Absolutely."

"I like you, Reed." She put her hand over his, friend to friend. "It's a pity you don't have more illusions."

He didn't ask her what she meant. He wasn't certain he wanted to know. Conversation stopped when the waiter arrived with menus and a list of specials delivered in a rolling French accent Maddy decided was genuine.

"This is a problem," Maddy muttered when they were alone again.

Reed glanced up from his menu. "You don't like French food?"

"Are you kidding?" She grinned at him. "I love it. I love Italian food, Armenian food, East Indian food. That's the problem."

"You suggested pizza," he reminded her. "It's hard to believe you're worried about calories."

"I was only going to have one piece and inhale the rest." She caught her bottom lip between her teeth and knew she could have eaten anything on the menu. "I have two choices. I can order just a salad and deny myself. Or I can say this is a celebration and shoot the works."

"I can recommend the *côtelettes de saumon*."

She lifted her gaze from the menu again to study him very seriously. "You can?"

"Highly."

"Reed, I'm a grown woman and independent by nature. When it comes to food, however, I often have the appetite of a twelve-year-old in a bakery. I'm going to put myself in your hands." She closed the menu and set it aside. "With the stipulation that you understand I can only eat this way once or twice a year unless I want to bounce around stage like a meatball."

"Understood." He decided, for reasons he didn't delve into, to give her the meal of her life.

He wasn't disappointed. Her unabashed appreciation for everything put in front of her was novel and
somehow compelling. She ate slowly, with a dark,
sensual enjoyment Reed had forgotten could be found
in food. She tasted everything and finished nothing,
and it was clear that the underlying discipline was always there, despite her sumptuous appreciation.

She teased herself with flavors as other women
might tease themselves with men. She closed her eyes
over a bite of fish and gave herself to the pleasure of
it as others gave themselves to the pleasures of lovemaking.

Champagne bubbles exploded in their glasses, and
the scents rising up were rich.

"Oh, this is wonderful. Taste."

Wanting to share her pleasure, she held her fork out
to him. His body tightened, surprising him. He had
been aroused just by watching her, but he discovered
in that instant that what he really wanted was to sam-
ple her, slowly, as she sampled the tastes and textures
on her plate.

He opened his mouth and allowed himself to be fed.
As he savored the bite, he watched her eyes and saw
they were aware. Mixed with that awareness was a curiosity that became intensely erotic.

"It's very good."

She knew she was getting in over her head, and she
wondered why the feeling was so alluring. "Dancers
think about food too much. I suppose it's because we
watch so much of it pass us by."

"You said once that dancers are always hungry."

He wasn't speaking of food now. To give herself a
moment, Maddy picked up her glass and sipped. "We
make a choice, usually in childhood. We give up foot-

ball games, TV, parties, and go to class instead. It carries over into adulthood.''

''How much do you sacrifice?''

''Whatever it takes.''

''And it's worth it?''

''Yes.'' She smiled, more comfortable now that she could feel her body pull away from that trembling edge of tension. ''Even at its worst, it's worth it.''

He leaned back just enough to distance himself from her. She sensed it and wondered whether he had felt the same intensity between them. ''What does success mean to you?''

''When I was sixteen, it meant Broadway.'' She looked around the quiet restaurant and nearly sighed. ''In some ways, it still does.''

''Then you have it.''

He didn't understand, nor did she expect him to. ''I feel successful because I tell myself the show's going to be a smash. I don't let myself think it might flop.''

''You wear blinders, then.''

''Oh, no. Rose-colored glasses, but never blinders. You're a realist. I suppose I like that in you because it's so different from what I am. I like to pretend.''

''You can't run a business on illusions.''

''And your personal life?''

''That either.''

Interested, she leaned forward. ''Why not?''

''Because you can only make things work your way if you know what's real and what's not.''

''I like to think you can make things real.''

''Valentine!''

Reed's considering frown lingered as he glanced up at a tall, lanky man in a peach jacket and a melon tie. ''Selby. How are you?''

"Fine. Just fine." The man sent Maddy a long look. "It looks like I'm interrupting, and I hate to use a tired line, but have we met before?"

"No." Maddy extended her hand with the easy friendship she showed everyone.

"Maddy O'Hurley. Allen Selby."

"Maddy O'Hurley?" Selby cut into Reed's introduction and squeezed Maddy's hand. "This is a pleasure. I saw *Suzanna's Park* twice."

She didn't like the feel of his hand, but she always hated herself when she made snap judgments. "Then it's my pleasure."

"I'd heard Valentine was dipping into Broadway, Reed."

"Word gets around." Reed poured the last of the wine into Maddy's glass. "Allen is the head of Galloway Records."

"Friendly competitors," Selby assured her, and Maddy got the distinct impression that he'd cut Reed's professional throat at the first opportunity. "Have you ever considered a solo album, Maddy?"

She toyed with the stem of her glass. "It's a difficult thing to admit to a record producer, but singing's not my strong point."

"If Reed doesn't convince you differently, come see me." He laid a hand on Reed's shoulder as he spoke. No, she didn't like those hands, she thought again. It couldn't be helped. Maddy noticed that Reed's eyes frosted over, but he merely picked up his glass. "Wish I could join you for some coffee," Selby went on, ignoring the fact he hadn't been asked, "but I'm meeting a client for dinner. Give my best to your old man, Reed. Think about that album now." He winked at Maddy, then sauntered off to his own table.

Maddy waited a beat, then finished off the rest of her wine. "Do most record producers dress like they're part of a fruit salad?"

Reed stared at her a moment, seeing the bland, curious smile. The tension dissolved into laughter. "Selby's one of a kind."

She took his hand again, delighted to have made him laugh. "So are you."

"Do I need time to decide if that was a compliment or an insult?"

"A definite compliment." She glanced over to where Selby was signaling a waiter. "You don't like him."

He didn't pretend not to understand who she was referring to. "We're business rivals."

"No," Maddy said with a shake of her head. "You don't like *him*. Personally."

That interested him, because he had a well-earned reputation for concealing his emotions. "Why do you say that?"

"Because your eyes iced over." Involuntarily she shivered. "I'd hate to be looked at that way. Anyway, you won't gossip, and you're annoyed that he's here, so why don't we go?"

When they walked outside again, the heat of the day had eased. Traffic had thinned. Hooking her arm through his, Maddy breathed in the rough night air that was New York. "Can we walk awhile? It's too nice to jump right into a cab."

They strolled down the sidewalk, past dark store windows and closed shops. "Selby had a point, you know. With the right material, you could make a very solid album."

She shrugged. That had never been part of her dream, though she wouldn't completely dismiss it. "Maybe someday, but I think Streisand can sleep easy. You never see enough stars," she murmured, looking up as they walked. "On nights like this I envy Abby and her farm in the country."

"Difficult to sit on the porch swing and make the eight-o'clock curtain."

"Exactly. Still, I keep planning to take this wonderful vacation some day. A cruise on the South Seas where the steward brings you iced tea while you watch the moon hovering over the water. Or a cabin in the woods—Oregon, maybe—where you can lie in bed in the morning and listen to the birds wake up. Trouble is, how would I make it to dance class?" She laughed at herself and moved closer. "What do you do when you have time off, Reed?"

It had been two years since he'd taken anything more than a long weekend off, and even those were few and far between. It had been two years since he'd taken over Valentine Records. "We have a house in St. Thomas. You can sit on the balcony and forget there is a Manhattan."

"It must be wonderful. One of those big, rambling places, pink-and-white stucco with a garden full of flowers most people only see in pictures. But you'd have phones. A man like you would never really cut himself off."

"Everyone pays a price."

She knew that very well every time she placed her hand on the *barre*. "Oh, look." She stopped by a window and looked in at an icy-blue negligee that swept the mannequin's feet and left the shoulders bare but for ivory lace. "That's Chantel."

Reed studied the faceless mannequin. "Is it?"

"The negligee. It's Chantel. Cool and sexy. She was born to wear things like that—and she's the first one to say so." Maddy laughed and stepped back to make a note of the name of the shop. "I'll have to send it to her. Our birthday's in a couple of months."

"Chantel O'Hurley." Reed shook his head. "Strange, I never put it together. She's your sister."

"Not so strange. We're not a great deal alike on the surface."

Cool and sexy, Reed thought again. That was precisely Chantel's image as a symbol of Hollywood glamour. The woman beside him would never be termed cool, and her sexuality wasn't glamorous but tangible. Dangerously so. "Being a triplet must be a very unique sensation."

"It's hard for me to say, since I've always been one." They began to walk again. "But it's special. You're never really alone, you know. I think that was part of the reason I had enough courage to come to New York and risk it all. I always had Chantel and Abby, even when they were hundreds of miles away."

"You miss them."

"Oh, yes. I miss them dreadfully sometimes, and Mom and Pop and Trace. We were so close growing up, living in each other's pockets, working together. Yelling at each other."

She chuckled when he glanced down at her. "It's not so odd, you know. Everyone needs someone they can yell at now and then. When Trace left, it was like losing an arm at first. Pop never really got over it. Then Abby left, and Chantel and I. I never thought how hard it was on my parents, because they had each other. You must be close to your parents."

He closed up then, instantly; she thought she could feel the frost settle over the heat. "There's only my father."

"I'm sorry." She never deliberately opened old wounds, but innate curiosity often led her to them. "I've never lost anyone close to me, but I can imagine how hard it would be."

"My mother's not dead." He didn't accept sympathy. He detested it.

Questions sprang into her head, but she didn't ask them. "Your father's a wonderful man. I could tell right away. He has such kind eyes. I always loved that about my own father—the way his eyes would say 'Trust me,' and you knew you could. My mother ran away with him, you know. It always seemed so romantic. She was seventeen and had already been working clubs for years. My father came through town and promised her the moon on a silver platter. I don't think she ever believed him, but she went with him. When we were little, my sisters and I used to talk about the day a man would come and offer us the moon."

"Is that what you want?"

"The moon?" She laughed again, and the sound of it trailed down the sidewalk. "Of course. And the stars. I might even take the man."

He stopped then, just outside the beam of a streetlight, to look down at her. "Any man who'd give it to you?"

"No." Her heart began to thud, slowly at first, then faster, until she felt it in her throat. "A man who'd offer it."

"A dreamer." He combed his hand through her hair the way he'd wanted to, though he'd told himself he wouldn't. It spread like silk through his fingers. "Like you."

"If you stop dreaming, you stop living."

He shook his head, moving it closer to hers. "I stopped a long time ago." His lips touched hers, briefly, as they had once before. "I'm still alive."

She put a hand on his chest, not to keep him away but to keep him close. "Why did you stop?"

"I prefer reality."

This time, when his mouth came to hers, it wasn't hesitant. He gathered and took what he'd wanted for days. Her lips were warm against his, exotic in flavor, tempting in their very willingness to merge with his. Her hand pressed against the back of his neck, drawing him nearer, eagerly accepting the next stage of pleasure as their tongues met and tangled.

The streetlight washed the sidewalk beside them, and the buildings blocked out most of the sky. They were alone, though traffic shuttled by on the street. His fingers spread against her back, bringing enough pressure to align her body with his, hard and firm. The scent she wore made the musky smell of the city disappear, so there was only her.

Trapped in his arms, she was already soaring up so that in a moment she could touch the chilled white surface of the moon and learn its secrets. She hadn't expected to be breathless, but she swayed against him with a helplessness neither of them could comprehend.

He tasted of power and ruthlessness. Her instinct for survival should have had her turning away from it, even scorning it. Yet she remained as she was, wound around him in the warm evening air. The hand at the back of his neck stroked to soothe a tension she sensed intuitively.

He knew better. From the first moment he'd seen her, Reed had known better. But he'd continued to take steps toward her rather than away. He was no good for her, and she could only mean catastrophe for him. There would be no casually complementary relationship here, but something that would draw you farther and farther into a slowly burning fire.

He could taste it. The frank surrender that was seduction. He could hear it in her quiet sigh of acceptance. With her body hugged tightly against his, he could feel the need expand beyond what should, what must, be controlled. He didn't want it. Yet he wanted her more than he'd wanted anything that had come into his life before.

He drew away. Then, before he could stop himself, he framed her face in his hands to kiss her again. He wanted to be sated by her, done with her. But the more he took, the more he wanted.

A woman like this could destroy a man. Since childhood his life had been based on the premise that he would never allow a woman to be important enough to hurt him. Maddy was no different, he told himself as he all but drowned in her. She couldn't be.

When he drew away again, Maddy's legs were rubber. She had no flip remark, no easy smile. She could only look into his eyes, and what she saw wasn't passion now, wasn't desire. It was anger. She had no answer for it.

"I'll take you home," he told her.

"Just a minute." She needed to catch her breath, needed to feel firm ground under her feet again. He released her, and she stepped to the street lamp and rested a hand on the solid metal surface. Light washed white over her and left him in shadow. "I get the feeling that you're annoyed at what happened."

He didn't respond. When she studied him, she saw that his eyes could be colder than stone. It made her hurt, as much for him as for herself. "Since I'm not, I'm left feeling like a fool." Tears came to her easily, as easily as laughter, but she wouldn't shed them now. She'd inherited a good deal of pride as well as quick emotions from her parents. "I'd just as soon see myself home, thanks."

"I said I'd take you."

Inner strength came back. It might have been the underlying fury in his voice that did it. "I'm a big girl, Reed. I've been responsible for myself a long time. See you around."

Maddy walked to the corner and lifted a hand. Fate took pity on her and sent a cab steering toward the curb. She got in without looking back.

He stood there until he saw her get safely inside. Then he stood there longer. He'd done them both a favor—that was what he told himself. He continued to tell himself that over and over as he remembered how soft and fragile she'd looked in the bright glow of the streetlight.

Turning away, he began to walk. It was late before he headed for home.

Chapter Five

Maddy stood stage left and took her cue from Wanda. There was no audience, but the theater was far from empty. The rest of the dancers were positioned across the stage, and Macke stood at the front, ready to dissect every move. In addition, there were the stage manager, the lighting director, their assistants, the accompanist—with the composer standing nervously close by, along with several technicians and the one who would make it all work—the director.

"Listen, honey," Wanda began, in character as Maureen Core, a fellow stripper, "this guy's a pipe dream. You're asking for trouble."

"He's an answer," Maddy shot back, and crossed to an imaginary bar on the empty stage. She poured herself an invisible drink, tossed it back and grinned. "He's the ticket I've been standing in line for all of my life."

"Get it in diamonds, babe." Wanda walked toward her, running her fingers up her arm as if she were enjoying the sensuous feel of a diamond bracelet. "And put them in a nice dark safe deposit box, 'cause when he finds out what you are he's going to be gone before you can shake your—"

"He's not going to find out," Maddy told her. "He's never going to find out. You think a class act like him is ever going to find his way to a dump like this?" She cast a disdainful look around the empty stage. "I tell you, Maureen, I've got a chance. For the first time in my life, I've got a chance."

The accompanist gave her her intro, and Maddy's mind went blank.

"Maddy." The director, known more for his skill than his patience, snapped her back. She swore with the ripe expertise she reserved solely for foul ups on stage.

"Sorry, Don."

"You're only giving me about fifty percent, Maddy. I need a hundred and ten."

"You'll get it." She rubbed at the tension in her neck. "Give me a minute first, will you?"

"Five," he said, clipping off the word so that the dancers shifted uneasily before they dispersed. Maddy walked off stage left and dropped down on a box in the wings.

"Problem?" Wanda sat down beside her, casting a look around designed to keep anyone else at a safe distance.

"I hate to mess up."

"I make it a policy to keep my nose out of other people's business. But . . ."

"There's always a but."

"You've been walking around on three cylinders for about a week. I'd say you're due for a tune-up."

She couldn't deny it; she didn't try to. Instead, she set her jaw on her hand. "Why are men such jerks?"

Wanda considered a moment. "Same reason the sky's blue, honey. They were made that way."

Another time, she might have laughed. Now she only nodded grimly. "I guess it's smarter just to leave them alone."

"A hell of a lot smarter," Wanda agreed. "Not much fun, but smarter. Your guy giving you trouble?"

"He's not my guy." Maddy sighed and frowned down at her shoe. "But he's giving me trouble. What do you do when a man kisses you as though he'd like to nibble away at you for the next twenty years, then brushes you aside as though you were never really there in the first place?"

Wanda cupped a hand around her instep, then brought her leg up to keep the muscles limber. "Well, you can forget him. Or you can give him another chance to nibble until he's hooked."

"I don't want to hook anybody," Maddy mumbled.

"But you are," Wanda put in, stretching the other leg. "Hooked and dangling."

"I know." Misery was something completely foreign to her. She tried to shake it off, but it clung. "The problem is, I think he knows, too, and he doesn't want any part of it."

"Maybe you should think about what you want first."

"Yeah, but first you have to know what that is."

"Is it him?"

Maddy gave a sulky shrug and hated herself for being petulant. "It might be."

"Take a lesson from Mary on this one." Wanda gave her advice as she rose into a *plié.* "Go after what's good for you."

It sounded so easy. Maddy knew better than most how it was to get to what was good for you. "You know the problem with being a dancer, Wanda?"

Two members of the chorus, currently in the midst of a blistering affair, began to argue with low, steady malice. Wanda eavesdropped without a qualm. "I can name a couple hundred, but go ahead."

"You never have time to learn how to be just a person. When other girls were out snuggling at the drive-in with their boyfriends, we were sleeping so we could get up and go to class the next morning. I don't know what to do about him."

"Get in his way."

"Get in his way?"

"That's right. Get in his way enough and he'll end up doing it to himself."

Laughing, Maddy took her own chin in her hand. "Does this look irresistible?"

"Never know unless you try."

Maddy's fingers stroked down her chin. Then she dropped her hand. "You're right." She stood then, nodding. "You're absolutely right. Let's go. I think I'm ready to give Don a hundred and ten percent."

They ran through the dialogue again, but this time Maddy used her own nerves to give an edge to her character. When the accompanist cued her for the song, she poured herself into it. Part of the staging called for her to go toe-to-toe with Wanda. When she did, the other's dancer's eyes glittered with a combination of appreciation and approval that had Maddy's adrenaline soaring higher.

She was all over the stage during the chorus, interacting with the other dancers, moving so quickly that the intense control she kept on her breathing went unnoticed. She whirled to stage center, threw out her arms—selling it, as her father had shown her years before—and let the last note ring out.

Someone threw her a towel.

They went over the scene again and again, sharpening, making a few changes in the blocking. The lighting director and the stage manager went into a huddle, and then they went through it again. Satisfied—for the moment—they walked through the next scene. Maddy took a break, downed a pint of orange juice and a carton of yogurt, then went back for more.

It was twilight when she left the theater. A group of dancers were going to a local restaurant to unwind and recharge. Normally Maddy would have tagged along, content to remain in their company. Tonight, she felt she had two choices. She could go home and collapse in a hot tub, or she could get in Reed's way.

Going home was smarter. The last run-through had drained her store of energy. In any case, a woman who pursued an uninterested man—or a man who pursued an unwilling woman—showed a remarkable lack of good sense.

There were plenty of other people, people who had her own interests and ambitions, who would make less complicated companions. It wasn't as though men looked at her and ran in the other direction. She was well liked by most, she was usually appreciated for what she was, and if she really wanted to she could find an easy dinner partner and while away an enjoyable evening.

She went to five phone booths before she found one with its phone book still attached. Just checking, she told herself as she looked up Reed's name. It never hurt to check.

More than likely he lived way uptown. She'd just have to forgo her impulsive visit until she wasn't so tired. Her heart sank just a little when she found his address. He lived uptown, all right. Central Park West. There were nearly fifty blocks between them, fifty blocks that meant a great deal more than linear distance.

When she closed the phone book, it didn't occur to her that she could have lived there as well. She couldn't live there because she didn't understand Central Park West. She understood the Village, she understood SoHo, she understood the lower forties and the theater district.

She and Reed had nothing in common, and it was foolish to think otherwise. She began to walk, telling herself that she was going home, getting into the tub, climbing into bed with a book. She reminded herself that she'd never wanted a man in her life anyway. They expected things. They complicated things. She had dozens of dance routines filed in her head. There wasn't enough room left to let her think about a relationship.

Maddy went down into the subway, merging with the crowd. After a search, she unearthed a token from the bottom of her bag. Still lecturing herself, she went through the turnstile that would take her to the uptown train.

It would have been smarter to call first, Maddy decided as she stood on the sidewalk in front of the tall, intimidating building where Reed made his home. He might not be there. She paced down the sidewalk and back again. Worse, he might be there, but not alone. A woman in raw silk slacks strolled by with a pair of poodles and never gave Maddy a glance.

That was what this neighborhood was, she thought. Silk slacks and poodles. She was a mongrel in denim. She glanced down at her own roomy jeans and worn sneakers. At least she should have had the foresight to go home and change first.

Listen to yourself, Maddy ordered. You're standing here complaining about clothes. That's Chantel's line, it's never been yours. Besides, they're good enough for you. They're good enough for the people you know. If they're not good enough for Reed Valentine, what are you doing here?

I don't know, she mused. I'm an idiot.

No argument there.

Taking a deep breath, she walked forward through the wide glass doors into the quiet, marble-floored lobby.

She'd been an actress for years. Maddy put on an easy smile, tossed back her hair, then strolled over to the uniformed man behind the oak counter. "Hello. Is Reed in? Reed Valentine?"

"I'm sorry, miss. He hasn't come in yet this evening."

"Oh." She struggled not to let the depth of her disappointment show. "Well, I just dropped by."

"I'd be happy to take a message. Miss—" When he looked at her, really looked, his eyes widened. "You're Maddy O'Hurley."

She blinked. It was a very rare thing for her to be recognized outside the theater. Maddy knew better than anyone how different she appeared onstage. "Yes." She offered her hand automatically. "How do you do?"

"Oh, what a pleasure this is." The man, not much taller than she and twice as wide, took her hand in both of his. "When my wife wanted a treat for our anniversary, the kids got us two tickets for *Suzanna's Park*. Orchestra seats, too. What an evening we had."

"That's lovely." Maddy glanced at his name tag. "You must have wonderful children, Johnny."

"They're good sports. All six of them." He grinned at Maddy, showing one gold tooth. "Miss O'Hurley, I can't tell you how much we enjoyed watching you. My wife said it was like watching a sunrise."

"Thank you." Compliments like that one made the years of classes, the days and weeks of rehearsals, the cramped muscles, worthwhile. "Thank you very much."

"You know that part—Lord, my wife cried buckets—when you think Peter's gotten on the train, you think he's gone, and all the lights come down, with just that pale, pale blue one on you. And you sing, ah..." He cleared his throat. "How can he go," he began in a shaky baritone, "with my love wrapped around him?"

"How can he go," Maddy continued in a strong, vibrant contralto, "with my heart in his hand? I only know that I gave him a choice. And he didn't choose me."

"That's the one." Johnny shook his head and sighed. "I have to admit it brought a tear to my eye, too."

"I'm in a new musical that's scheduled to open in about six weeks."

"Are you now?" He beamed at her like a proud father. "We won't miss it, I promise you."

Maddy took a pencil from the counter and scrawled the name of the theater and the assistant stage manager on a pad. "You call this number, ask for Fred here and give my name. I'll see to it that you have two tickets for opening night."

"Opening night." His look of astonished pleasure was enough to warm Maddy all over. "My wife's not going to believe me. I don't know how to thank you, Miss O'Hurley."

She grinned at him. "Applaud."

"You can count on that. We'll— Oh, good evening, Mr. Valentine."

Maddy straightened from the counter like a shot, feeling guilty for no reason she could fathom. She turned and managed a smile. "Hello, Reed."

"Maddy." He'd come in during the brief duet, but neither of them had noticed.

When he only stared at her, she cleared her throat and decided to wing it. "I was up this way and decided to drop in and say hello. Hello."

He'd just come out of a long meeting where thoughts of her had distracted him. He wasn't pleased to see her. But he wanted to touch her. "Are you on your way somewhere?"

She could try being casually chic and lie about a party around the corner. She could just as easily grow a second head. "No. Just here."

Taking her by the arm, Reed nodded at Johnny, then led her to the elevators. "Are you always so generous with strangers?'' he asked as they stepped inside.

"Oh.'' After a moment's thought, she shrugged. "I suppose. You look a little tired.'' And wonderful, she added silently. Just wonderful.

"Long day.''

"Me too. We had our first full rehearsal today. It was a zoo.'' Then she laughed, nervously dipping her hands in her pockets. "I guess I shouldn't say that to the man with the checkbook.''

With an unintelligible mutter, he led her out into the hallway. Maddy decided silence was the best tack. Then he unlocked his door and brought her inside.

She'd expected something grand, something elegant, something tasteful. It was all that and more. When the lights were switched on, there was a feeling of space. The walls were pale, set off by vibrant impressionist paintings and three tall, wide windows that let in a lofty view of the park and the city. The pewter-toned rug was the perfect contrast to the long, spreading coral sofa. Two lush ficus trees stood in the corner, and set in two wall niches were the Ming vases she'd once imagined. A curved, open staircase led to a loft.

There wasn't a thing out of place, but she hadn't expected there to be. Still, it wasn't cold, and she hadn't been sure about that.

"It's lovely, Reed.'' She crossed to the windows to look down. If there was a problem, she felt it was here. He kept himself so aloof, so distant from the city he lived in, away from the sounds, the smells, the humanity of it. "Do you ever stand here and wonder what's going on?''

"What's going on where?''

"Down there, of course." She turned back to him with a silent invitation to join her. When he did, she looked down again. "Who's arguing, who's laughing, who's making love. Where's the police car going, and will he get there in time. How many street people will sleep in the park tonight. How many tricks turned, how many bottles opened, how many babies born. It's an incredible place, isn't it?"

She wore the same scent, light, teasing only because it was so guileless. "Not everyone looks at it the way you do."

"I always wanted to live in New York." She stepped back so that there were only lights, just the dazzle of them. "Ever since I can remember. It's strange how the three of us—my sisters, I mean—seemed to have this gut instinct where we belonged. As close as we are, we all chose completely different places. Abby's in rural Virginia, Chantel's in fantasyland, and I'm here."

He had to stop himself from stroking her hair. There was always that trace of wistfulness when she spoke of her sisters. He didn't understand family. He had only his father. "Would you like a drink?"

It was in his tone, the distance, the formality. She tried not to let it hurt. "I wouldn't mind some Perrier."

When he went to the compact ebony bar, she moved away from the window. She couldn't stand there, thinking about people milling around together, when she felt so divorced from the man she had come to see.

Then she saw the plant. He'd set it on a little stand where it would get indirect sunlight from the windows. The soil, when she tested it with her thumb, was moist but not soaking. She smiled as she touched a leaf. He could care, if only he allowed himself to.

"It looks better," Maddy said as she took the glass he offered.

"It's pitiful," Reed corrected, swirling the brandy in his snifter.

"No, really, it does. It doesn't look so, well...pale, I guess. Thank you."

"You were drowning it." He drank, and wished her eyes weren't so wide, so candid. "Why don't you sit down, Maddy? You can tell me why you came."

"I just wanted to see you." For the first time, she wished she had some of Chantel's flair with men. "Look, I'm lousy at this sort of thing." Unable to keep still, she began to wander around the apartment. "I never had time to develop a lot of style, and I only say clever lines when they're fed to me. I wanted to see you." Defiantly she sat on the edge of the sofa. "So I came."

"No style." It amazed him that he could be amused when this unwanted need for her was knotting his gut. "I see." He sat, as well, keeping a cushion between them. "Did you come to proposition me?"

Temper flared in her eyes and came out unexpectedly as hauter. "I see dancers don't have a patent on ego. I suppose the women you're used to are ready to tumble into bed when you crook your finger."

The smile threatened again as he lifted his brandy. "The women I'm used to don't sing duets in the lobby with the security guard."

She slammed down her glass, and the fizzing water plopped dangerously close to the rim. "Probably because they have tin ears."

"That's a possibility. The point is, Maddy, I don't know what to do about you."

"Do about me?" She rose, completely graceful, totally livid. "You don't have to do *anything* about me. I don't want you to do anything about me. I'm not an Eliza Doolittle."

"You even think in plays."

"What if I do? You think in columns." Disgusted, she began to pace again. "I don't know what I'm doing here. It was stupid. Damn it, I've been miserable for a week. I'm not used to being miserable." She whirled back, accusing. "I missed my cue because I was thinking about you."

"Were you?" He rose, though he'd promised himself he wouldn't. He knew he should see to it that she was angry enough to leave before he did something he'd regret. But he was doing it now, moving closer to brush his thumb over her cheek.

"Yes." Desire rose and anger drained. She didn't know how to make room for both. She took his wrist before he could drop his hand. "I wanted you to think of me."

"Maybe I was." He wanted to gather her close, to feel her hard against him and pretend for just a little while. "Maybe I caught myself looking out the window of my office and wondering about you."

She rose on her toes to meet his lips. There was a storm brewing in him, she could feel it. She had storms of her own, but she knew his would be for different reasons and have different results. Was it necessary to understand him, when being with him felt so right? It was enough for her. But even as she thought it, she knew it would never be enough for him.

"Reed—"

"No." His hands were hard and tense on her back, in her hair, as he pulled her closer. "Don't talk now."

He needed what she could give him, with her mouth, with her arms, with the movement of her body against his. His home had never seemed empty until she had come into his life. Now that she was here, with him, he didn't want to think about being alone again.

Her mouth was like velvet, warm and smooth, as comforting as it was arousing. When she touched him, it felt as though she wanted to give, rather than take. For a moment he could almost believe it.

How easily he could lure her under. A kiss had always been a simple thing to her. Something to show affection to a loved one with, something to be given casually to a friend, even something to be played up onstage for a theater full of people. But with Reed, the simplicity ended. This was complex, overwhelming, a contact that shot sparks through every nerve ending. Passion wasn't new to her. She experienced it every day in her work. She'd known that it was different when it involved a man and woman, but she hadn't realized it could turn her muscles to water and cloud her brain.

He ran his hands through her hair. She wished he would move them over her, over every inch of the body that throbbed and ached for him. He wanted her. She could taste the frenzied desire every time his mouth met hers. Yet he did nothing more than hold her close against him.

Make love with me, her mind requested, but her lips were captured by his and couldn't form the words. She could picture candlelight, soft music and a big, wide bed with the two of them tangled together. The image made her skin heat and her mouth more aggressive.

"Reed, do you want me?"

Even as her mouth skimmed over his face, she felt him stiffen. Just slightly, but she felt it. "Yes."

It was the way he said it that cooled her blood. Reluctance, even annoyance, glazed over the answer. Maddy drew away slowly. "You have a problem with that?"

Why couldn't it be as simple with her as it was with other women? Mutual enjoyment, rules up front, and nobody's hurt. He'd known from the first time he'd touched her that it wouldn't be simple with her. "Yes." He went back for his brandy, hoping it would steady him. "I have a problem with that."

She was going too fast, Maddy decided. It was a bad habit of hers to move at top speed without looking for the bumps in the road. "Would you like to share it with me?"

"I want you." The statement wiped away what she'd hoped was a casual smile. "I've wanted to take you to bed since I watched you gathering up loose change and sweaty clothes off the sidewalk."

She took a step closer. Did he know that was what she'd wanted to hear, even though it frightened her a little? Did he know how much she wanted him to feel some portion of what she felt? "Why did you send me away the other night?"

"I'm no good for you, Maddy."

She stared at him. "Wait a minute. I want to be sure I understand this. You sent me away for my own good."

He splashed more brandy into the glass. It wasn't helping. "That's right."

"Reed, you make a child wear scratchy clothes in the winter for her own good. Once she gets past a certain age, she's on her own."

He wondered how in the hell he was supposed to argue with an analogy like that. "You don't strike me as the kind of woman interested in one-night stands."

Her smile chilled. "No, I'm not."

"Then I did you a favor." He drank again because he was beginning to despise himself.

"I guess I should say thank you." She picked up her dance bag, then dropped it again. It just wasn't an O'Hurley trait to give up easily. "I want to know why you're so sure it would have been a one-night stand."

"I'm not interested in the long term."

She nodded, telling herself that was reasonable. "There's a big difference between one night and the long term. I get the feeling that you think I'm trying to put a cage around you."

She didn't know that the cage was half formed already, and that he'd built it himself. "Maddy, why don't we just leave it that you and I have nothing in common."

"I've thought about that." Now that she had something solid to dig her teeth into, she relaxed again. "It's true to a point, you know, but when you really think about it, we have plenty in common. We both live in New York."

Lifting a brow, he leaned back against the bar. "Of course. That wipes everything else out."

"It's a start." She caught it, that faint glimpse of amusement. It was enough for her. "We both, at the moment, have a vested interest in a certain musical."

She smiled at him, instinctively and irresistibly charming. "I put my socks on before my shoes. How about you?"

"Maddy—"

"Do you stand up in the shower?"

"I don't see—"

"Come on, no evasions. Just the truth. Do you?"

It was useless. He had to smile. "Yes."

"Amazing. So do I. Ever read *Gone with the Wind*?"

"Yes."

"Ah. Common ground in literature. I could probably go on for hours."

"I'm sure you could." He set his brandy down and went to her again. "What's the point, Maddy?"

"The point is, I like you, Reed." She put her hands on his forearms, wishing she could ease the tension and keep that smile in his eyes just a bit longer. "I think if you'd loosen up, just a little, we could be friends. I'm attracted to you. I think if we take our time we could be lovers, too."

It was a mistake, of course. He knew it, but she looked so appealing just then, so honest and carefree. "You are," he murmured as he toyed with a strand of her hair, "unique."

"I hope so." With a smile, she rose up on her toes and kissed him, without heat, without passion. "Is it a deal?"

"You might regret it."

"Then that's my problem, isn't it? Friends?" She offered her hand solemnly, but her eyes laughed at him, challenging.

"Friends," he agreed, and hoped he wouldn't be the one to regret it.

"Great. Listen, I'm starving. Have you got a can of soup or something?"

Chapter Six

On the surface, it appeared to be every bit as simple as Maddy had said it could be. For a great many people it would have been simple beneath the surface, as well. But not everyone wanted as deeply as Reed or pretended as well as Maddy.

They went to the movies. Whenever their schedules meshed and the weather cooperated, they had lunch in the Park. They spent one quiet Sunday afternoon wandering through a museum, more interested in each other than in the exhibits. If Reed hadn't known himself better, he would have said he was on the brink of having a romance. But he didn't believe in romance.

Love had brought his father betrayal, a betrayal Reed himself lived with every day. If Edwin had put it behind him, Reed had not, could not. Fidelity, to the majority of the people he worked with, was nothing if not flexible. People had affairs, not romances, and they had them before, during and after marriage, so that marriage itself was a moot point. Nothing lasted forever, particularly not relationships.

But he thought of Maddy when he wasn't with her, and he thought of little else when they were together.

Friends. Somehow they'd managed to become friends, despite their differing outlooks and opposite backgrounds. If the friendship was cautious on his part and careless on hers, they'd still found enough between them to form a base. Where did they go from here?

Lovers. It seemed inevitable that they would become lovers. The passion that simmered under the surface every moment they were together wouldn't be held back for long. They both knew it and, in their different ways, accepted it. What worried Reed was that once he'd taken her to bed, as he wanted to, he would lose the easy companionship he was coming to depend on.

Sex would change things. It was bound to. Intimacy on a physical level would jar the emotional intimacy they had just begun to develop. As much as he needed Maddy in his bed, he wondered if he could afford to risk losing the Maddy he knew out of bed. It was a tug-of-war he knew he could never really win.

Yet he didn't believe in losing. Given enough logical thought, enough planning, he should be able to find a way to have both. Did it matter if he was being calculating, even cold-blooded, when the end result would please both of them?

The answer wouldn't come. Instead, an image ran through his head of Maddy as she'd been a few afternoons before, laughing, tossing bread crumbs to pigeons in the Park.

When the buzzer sounded on his desk, he discovered he'd lost another ten minutes daydreaming. "Yes, Hannah."

"Your father's on line one, Mr. Valentine."

"Thank you." Reed pushed a button and made the connection. "Dad?"

"Reed, heard a rumor that Selby's taken on a fresh batch of indies. Know anything about it?"

Reed already had a preliminary report on the influx of independent record promoters taken on by Galloway. "Keeping your ear to the ground on the 'nineteenth' hole?"

"Something like that."

"There's talk of some pressure on some of the Top 40 stations to add a few records to their playlist. Nothing new. A few whispers of payola, but nothing that gels."

"Selby's a slippery sonofabitch. You hear anything concrete, I wouldn't mind being informed."

"You'll be the first."

"Never liked the idea of paying to have a record air," Edwin muttered. "Well, it's an old gambit, and I'm thinking more of new ones. I wanted to see a rehearsal of our play. Would you like to join me?"

Reed glanced at his desk calendar. "When?"

"In an hour. I know it's the form to let them know; they'd like to be on their toes when the bank roll's expected, but I like surprises."

Reed noted two appointments that morning and started to refuse. Giving in to impulse, he decided to reschedule. "I'll meet you at the theater at eleven."

"Stretch it into lunch? Your old man's buying."

He was lonely, Reed realized. Edwin Valentine had his club, his friends and enough money to cruise around the world, but he was lonely. "I'll bring an appetite," Reed told him, then hung up to juggle his schedule.

Edwin entered the theater stealthily, like a boy without a ticket. "We'll just slip into a seat on the aisle and see what we're paying for."

Reed walked behind his father, but his gaze was on the stage, where Maddy was wrapped in the arms of another man. He felt the lunge of jealousy, so surprisingly fierce that he stopped in the center of the aisle and stared.

She was looking up at another man, her arms linked behind his neck, her face glowing. "I really had a wonderful time, Jonathan. I could have danced forever."

"You're talking like it's over. We have hours yet." Reed watched as the man pressed a kiss to her forehead. "Come home with me."

"Come home with you?" Even with the distance, Reed could sense the alarm in the set of Maddy's body. "Oh, Jonathan, I'd like to, really." She drew away, just a little, but he caught her hands. "I just can't. I have to... I have to be at work early. Yes, that's it. And there's my mother." She turned away again, rolling her eyes so that the audience could see the lie while the man beside her couldn't. "She's not really well, you know, and I should be there in case she needs anything."

"You're such a good person, Mary."

"Oh, no." Guilt and distress were hinted at in her voice. "No, Jonathan, I'm not."

"Don't say that." He drew her into his arms again. "Because I think I'm falling in love with you."

She was caught up in another kiss. Even knowing it was only a play, Reed felt something twist in his stomach.

"I have to go," she said quickly. "I really have to." Pulling away, she darted across stage right.

"When will I see you again?"

She stopped and seemed at war within herself. "Tomorrow. Come to the library at six. I'll meet you."

"Mary—" He started toward her, but she held up both hands.

"Tomorrow," she said again, and ran offstage.

"All right." The director's voice boomed out. "We'll have fifteen seconds here for the drops and set change. Wanda, Rose, take your marks. Lights go on. Cue, Maddy."

She came rushing onstage again to where Wanda was lounging in a chair and the woman named Rose was primping in a mirror.

"You're late," Wanda said lazily.

"What are you, a time clock?" Maddy's voice had an edge of toughness now; her movements were sharper.

"Jackie was looking for you."

Maddy stopped in the act of pulling on a wild red wig. "What'd you tell him?"

"That he wasn't looking in the right places. Don't stretch your G-string, Mary. I covered for you."

"Yeah, she covered for you," Rose agreed, snapping a wad of gum and fussing with her outrageous pink-and-orange costume.

"Thanks." Maddy whipped off her skirt. Nudging Rose aside, she began to paint her face.

"Don't thank me. We gotta stick together." She watched negligently as Rose practiced a routine. "Think you're nuts, though," Wanda added.

"I know what I'm doing." Maddy slipped behind a screen. The blouse she'd worn flapped across it. "I can handle it."

"You better make sure you can handle Jackie. Any idea what he'd do to you and your pretty boy if he found out what's going on?"

"He's not going to find out." She came out from the screen in a long, slinky gown covered with red spangles. "Look, I'm on."

"Crowd's pretty hot tonight."

"Good." She sent Wanda a grin. "That's the way I like them." She walked off stage right again.

"Lights stage left," the stage manager called. "Cue Terry."

A dancer Reed recognized from the only other rehearsal he'd seen paced out on stage left. His hair was slicked back, and he'd added a pencil-thin moustache. He wore a brilliant white tie against a black shirt. When Maddy came out behind him, he grabbed her arm.

"Where the hell you been?"

"Around." Maddy pushed back the mane of red hair, then settled a hand saucily on her hip. "What's your problem?"

Edwin leaned over and whispered to Reed. "Doesn't look like the little lady who came into your office with a dead plant."

"No," Reed murmured as the two on stage argued. "It doesn't."

"She's going to be big, Reed. Very, very big."

He felt twin surges of pride and alarm and could explain neither of them. "Yes, I think she is."

"Look, sugar." Maddy gave her partner a pat on the cheek. "You want me to go strip or stay here and read you my diary?"

"Strip," Jackie ordered her.

"Yeah." Maddy tossed her head back. "That's what I do best."

"Lights," the stage manager called out. "Music."

Maddy grabbed a red boa and walked—no, sauntered—to center stage, then stood there like a flame. When she began to sing, her voice came slowly and built, as arousing and teasing as the movements she began to make. The boa was tossed into the audience. It would be replaced dozens of times before the play closed.

"I never took you to a strip joint, did I, Reed?"

He had to smile, even as Maddy began to peel off elbow-length gloves. "No, you didn't."

"Hole in your education."

Onstage, Maddy let her body take over. It was just one routine among nearly a dozen others, but she knew it had the potential to be a showstopper if she played it right. She intended to.

When she whipped off the skirt of the dress, some of the technicians began to whistle. She grinned and went into a series of thunderous bumps and grinds. When the two-minute dance had run its course, she sat on the stage, arched back, wearing little more than spangles and beads. To her surprise and pleasure, there was a smattering of applause from the center of the audience. Exhausted, she propped herself on her elbow and smiled out into the darkened theater.

Word traveled quickly, from assistant to assistant to stage manager to director. Money was in the house.

Don went down the aisle, swearing because the grapevine hadn't gotten to him sooner. "Mr. Valentine. And Mr. Valentine." He offered hearty handshakes. "We weren't expecting you."

"We thought we'd catch something a little impromptu." Reed spoke to him, but his gaze wandered back to the stage, where Maddy still sat, dabbing at her throat now with a towel. "Very impressive."

"We could be a little sharper yet, but we'll be ready for Philadelphia."

"No doubt about that." Edwin gave him a friendly slap on the shoulder. "We don't want to hold things up."

"I'd love you to stay longer, if you could. We're about to rehearse the first scene from the second act. Please, come down front."

"Up to you, Reed."

He was going to have to put in an extra two hours with paperwork to make up for this. But he wasn't going to miss it. "Let's go."

The next scene was played strictly for laughs. Reed didn't know enough to dissect the comedic timing, the pacing, the stage business that made the simplest things funny. He could see, however, that Maddy knew how to play it to the hilt. She was going to have the audience eating out of her hand.

There was something vivid about her, something convincing and sympathetic even in her role as the brazen, somewhat edgy stripper. Reed watched her play two roles, adding the innocence necessary to convince the eager and honest Jonathan that his Mary was a dedicated librarian with a sick mother. He'd have believed her himself. And it was that quality that began to worry him.

"She's quite a performer," Edwin commented when the director and stage manager went into a huddle.

"Yes, she is."

"I suppose it's none of my business, but what's going on between you?"

Reed turned, his face expressionless. "What makes you think anything is?"

Edwin tapped the side of his nose. "I'd never have gotten this far in the business if I couldn't sniff things out."

"We're . . . friends," Reed said after a moment.

With a sigh, Edwin shifted his large bulk in the seat. "You know, Reed, one of the things I've always wanted for you is a woman like Maddy O'Hurley. A bright, beautiful woman who could make you happy."

"I am happy."

"You're still bitter."

"Not with you," Reed said immediately. "Never with you."

"Your mother—"

"Leave it." Though the words were quiet, the ice was there. "This has nothing to do with her."

It had everything to do with her, Edwin thought as Maddy took the stage again. But he knew his son well, and kept his silence.

Edwin couldn't turn back the clock and stop the betrayal. Even if it were possible, he wouldn't. If he could, and did, Reed wouldn't be sitting beside him now. How could he teach his son that it was a matter not of forgiveness but of acceptance? How could he teach him to trust when he'd been born of a lie?

Edwin studied Maddy as her bright, expressive face lighted the stage. Could she be the one to do the teaching?

Maybe she was the woman Reed had always needed, the answer he'd always searched for without acknowledging that he was looking. Maybe, through Maddy, Edwin could lay all his own past hurts to rest.

Even though it was simply a walk-through, Maddy kept the energy at a high level. She didn't believe in pacing herself through a performance, or through life, but in going full out and seeing where it landed her.

While she ran through her lines, practiced her moves, part of her concentration focused on Reed. He was watching her so intently. It was if he were trying to see through her role to who and what she really was. Didn't he understand that it was her job to submerge herself until there was no Maddy, only Mary?

She thought she sensed disapproval, even annoyance—a completely different mood from the one he'd sat down with. She wanted badly to jump down from the stage and somehow reassure him, though of what she wasn't sure. But he didn't want that from her. At least not yet. For now he wanted everything casual, very, very light. No strings, no promises, no future.

She stumbled over a line, swore at herself. They backtracked and began again.

She couldn't tell him how she felt. For a woman with an honest nature, even silence was deception. But she couldn't tell him. He didn't want to hear her say she loved him, had begun to love him from the moment she'd stood on the sidewalk with him at dusk. He would be angry, because he didn't want to be trapped by emotion. He wouldn't understand that she simply lived on emotion.

Perhaps he'd think she simply gave her love easily. It was true enough that she did, but not this kind of love. Love of family was natural and always there. Love of friends evolved slowly or quickly, but with no qualms. She could love a child in the park for nothing more than his innocence, or an old man on the street for nothing more than his endurance.

But loving Reed involved everything. This love was complex, and she'd always thought loving was simple. It hurt, and she'd always believed love brought joy. The passion was there, always simmering underneath. It made her restless with anticipation, when she'd always been so easygoing.

She'd invited him into her life. That was something she couldn't forget. More, she'd argued him into her life when he'd been ready to back away. So she loved him. But she couldn't tell him.

"Lunch, ladies and gentlemen. Be back at two, prepared to run through the two final scenes."

"So it's the angel," Wanda murmured in Maddy's ear. "The one in the front row who looks like a cover for *Gentleman's Quarterly*."

"What about him?" Maddy bent from the waist and let her muscles relax.

"That's him, isn't it?"

"What him?"

"*The* him." Wanda gave her a quick slap on the rump. "The him that's had you standing around dreamy eyed."

"I don't stand around dreamy eyed." At least she hoped she didn't.

"That's him," Wanda said with a self-satisfied smile before she strolled offstage.

Grumbling to herself, Maddy walked down the steps beside the stage. She put on a fresh smile. "Reed, I'm glad you came." She didn't touch him or offer the quick, friendly kiss she usually greeted him with. "Mr. Valentine. It's so nice to see you again."

"I enjoyed every minute of it." He sandwiched her hand between his big ones. "It's a pleasure to watch you work. Did I hear the man mention lunch?"

She put a hand on her stomach. "That you did."

"Then you'll join us, won't you?"

"Well, I..." When Reed said nothing, she searched for an excuse.

"Now, you wouldn't disappoint me." Edwin ignored his son's silence and barreled ahead. "This is your neck of the woods. You must know a good spot."

"There's a deli just across the street," she began.

"Perfect. I could eat a good pastrami." And it would only take a quick call to cancel his reservation at the Four Seasons. "What do you say, Reed?"

"I'd say Maddy needs a minute to change." He finally smiled at her.

She glanced down at her costume of hot-pink shorts and tank top. "Five minutes to get into my street clothes," she promised, and dashed away.

She was better than her word. Within five minutes she had thrown a yellow sweat suit over her costume and was walking into the deli in front of Reed and his father.

The smells were wonderful. There were times she stopped in for them alone. Spiced meat, hot mustard, strong coffee. An overhead fan stirred it all up. Most of the dancers had headed there from the theater like hungry ants to a picnic. Because the proprietor was shrewd, there was a jukebox in the rear corner. It was already blasting away.

The big Greek behind the counter spotted Maddy and gave her a wide white grin. "Ahhh, an O'Hurley special?"

"Absolutely." Leaning on the glass front of the counter, she watched him dish up a big, leafy salad. He used a generous hand with chunks of cheese, then topped it off with a dollop of yogurt.

"You eat that?" Edwin asked behind her.

She laughed and accepted the bowl. "I absorb it."

"Body needs meat." Edwin ordered a pastrami on a huge kaiser roll.

"I'll get us a table," Maddy offered, grabbing a cup of tea to go with the salad. Wisely she commandeered one on the opposite end of the room from the music.

"Lunch with the big boys, huh, Maddy?" Terry, with his hair still slicked back á la Jackie, stooped over her. "Going to put in a good word for me?"

"What word would you like?" She turned in her chair to grin up at him.

"How about 'star'?"

"I'll see if I can work it in."

He started to say something else but glanced over at his own table. "Damn it, Leroy, that's my pickle."

Maddy was still laughing when Reed and his father joined her.

"Quite a place," Edwin commented, already looking forward to his sandwich and the heap of potato salad beside it.

"They're on their best behavior because you're here."

Someone started to sing over the blare of the juke-box. Maddy simply pitched her voice higher. "Will you come to the Philadelphia opening, Mr. Valentine?"

"Thinking about it. Don't travel as much as I used to. There was a time when the head of a record company had to be out of town as much as he was in his office."

"Must have been exciting." She dipped into her salad and pretended she didn't envy Reed his pile of rare roast beef.

"Hotel rooms, meetings." He shrugged. "And I missed my boy." The look he gave Reed was both rueful and affectionate. "Missed too many ball games."

"You made plenty of them." Reed sliced off a corner of his sandwich and handed it to Maddy. It was a small, completely natural gesture that caught Edwin's eye. And his hope.

"Reed was top pitcher on his high school team."

Reed was shaking his head with a smile of his own when Maddy turned to him. "You played ball? You never told me." As soon as the words were out, she reminded herself he had no reason to tell her. There were dozens of other details about his life that he hadn't told her. "I never really understood baseball until I moved to New York," she went on quickly. "Then I caught a few Yankee games to see what the fuss was about. What was your ERA?"

He lifted a brow. "2.38."

It pleased her that he remembered. She rolled her eyes at his father. "Big-league material."

"So I always told him. But he wanted to work in the business."

"That's the big leagues, too, isn't it?" She nibbled on the portion of sandwich Reed had given her. "Most of us only look at the finished product, you know, the album we put on the turntable, the cassette we stick in the car stereo. I guess it's a long trip from sheet music to vinyl.''

"When you've got three or four days free," Edwin said with a laugh, "I'll fill you in."

"I'd like that." She drank her honeyed tea, knowing it would seep into her bloodstream and get her through the next four hours. "When we recorded the cast album for *Suzanna's Park*, I got a taste of it. I think the studio's so different from the stage. So, well...restricted." She swallowed lettuce. "Sorry."

"No need."

"A studio has certain restrictions," Reed put in. He took a sip of his coffee and discovered it was strong enough to melt leather. "On the other hand, there can be untold advantages. We can take that man behind the counter, put him in a studio and turn him into Caruso by pushing the right buttons."

Maddy digested that, then shook her head. "That's cheating."

"That's marketing," Reed corrected. "And plenty of labels do it."

"Does Valentine?"

He looked at her, and the gray eyes she'd admired from the beginning were direct. "No. Valentine was started with an eye toward quality, not quantity."

She slanted Edwin a wicked look. "But you were going to offer a recording contract to the O'Hurley Triplets."

Edwin added an extra dash of pepper to his sandwich. "You weren't quality?"

"We were...a slice above mediocre."

"A great deal above, if what I saw onstage this afternoon is any indication."

"I appreciate that."

"Do you get time for much socializing, Maddy?"

She plopped her chin on her hands. "Asking me for a date?"

He seemed taken aback, though only for an instant. Then he roared with laughter that caught the attention of everyone in the deli. "Damned if I wouldn't if I could drop twenty years. Quite a prize right here." He patted her hand, but looked at his son.

"Yes, she is," Reed said blandly.

"I'm thinking of giving a party," Edwin said on impulse. "Sending the play off to Philadelphia in style. What do you think, Maddy?"

"I think it's a great idea. Am I invited?"

"On the condition that you save a dance for me."

It was as easy for her to love the father as it was for her to love the son. "You can have as many as you like."

"I don't think I can keep up with you for more than one."

She laughed with him. When she picked up her tea, she saw that Reed was watching her again, coolly. The sense of disapproval she felt from him cut her to the bone.

"I, ah, I have to get back. There are some things I have to do before afternoon rehearsal."

"Walk the lady across the street, Reed. Your legs are younger than mine."

"Oh, that's all right." Maddy was already up. "I don't need—"

"I'll walk you over." Reed had her by the elbow.

She wouldn't make a scene. For the life of her she couldn't pinpoint why she wanted to so badly. Instead, she bent down and kissed Edwin's cheek. "Thanks for lunch."

She waited until they were outside before she spoke again. "Reed, I'm perfectly capable of crossing the street alone. Go back to your father."

"Do you have a problem?"

"Do *I* have a problem?" She pulled her arm away and glared at him. "Oh, I can't stand to hear you say that to me in that proper, politely curious voice." She started across the street at a jog.

"You have twenty minutes to get back." He caught her arm again.

"I said I had things to do."

"You lied."

In the center of the street, with the light turning yellow, she turned toward him again. "Then let's say I have better things to do. Better things than to sit there and be put under your intellectual microscope. What's wrong, don't you like the fact that I enjoy your father's company? Are you afraid I have designs on him?"

"Stop it." He gave her a jerk to get her moving as cars began to honk.

"You just don't like women in general, do you? You put us all in this big box that's labeled 'Not To Be Trusted.' I wish I knew why."

"Maddy, you're becoming very close to hysterical."

"Oh, I can get a lot closer," she promised with deadly sincerity. "You froze up. I saw you when I was onstage and you were watching me with that cold, measuring look in your eyes. It was as if you thought you were looking at me instead of the part I was playing—and you didn't want either of us to win.''

Because he recognized the glimmer of truth, he shifted away from it. "You're being ridiculous."

"I'm not." She shoved away from him again as they stood by the stage door. "I know when I'm being ridiculous, and in this instance I'm not. I don't know what ate away at you, Reed, but whatever it was, I'm sorry for it. I've tried not to let it bother me, I've tried not to let a lot of things bother me. But this is too much."

He took her by the shoulders and held her against the wall. "What is too much?"

"I saw your face when your father was talking about having a party, about me being there. Well, you don't have to worry, I won't come. I'll make an excuse."

"What are you talking about?" he demanded, spacing each word carefully.

"I didn't realize you'd be embarrassed being seen with me."

"Maddy—"

"No, it's understandable, isn't it?" she rushed on. "I'm just plain Maddy O'Hurley, no degrees behind the name, no pedigree in front of it. I got my high school diploma in the mail, and both my parents can trace their roots back to peasant stock in the south of Ireland."

He caught her chin in his hand. "The next time you take a side trip, leave me a map so I can keep up. I don't know what you're talking about."

"I'm talking about us!" she shouted. "I don't know why I'm talking about us, because there *is* no us. You don't want an us. You don't even want a you and me, really, so I don't—"

He cut her off, out of total frustration, by pressing his mouth over hers. "Shut up," he warned when she struggled to protest. "Just shut up a minute."

He filled himself on her. God, if she knew how frustrated he'd been watching her seduce an empty theater, how empty he'd felt sitting beside her, unable to touch her. The anger poured through. He'd hurt her. And would probably hurt her again. He no longer knew how to avoid it.

"Calm?" he asked when he let her speak again.

"No."

"All right, then, just be quiet. I don't know exactly what I was thinking while I was watching you on-stage. It's becoming a problem to think at all when I look at you."

She started to snap, then thought better of it. "Why?"

"I don't know. As for the other business, you are being ridiculous. I don't care if you got your education in a correspondence school or at Vassar. I don't care if your father was knighted or tried for grand larceny."

"Disturbing the peace," Maddy mumbled. "But that was only once—twice, I guess. I'm sorry." As the tears rolled out, she apologized again. "I'm really sorry. I hate this. I always get so churned up when I'm angry, and I can't stop."

"Don't." He brushed at her tears himself. "I haven't been completely fair with you. We really need to clear up what the situation between us is."

"Okay. When?"

"When don't you have a class at the crack of dawn?"

She sniffed and searched in her dance bag for a tissue. "Sunday."

"Saturday, then. Will you come to my place?" He brushed a thumb along her cheekbone. She was being reasonable, too reasonable, when he knew he couldn't promise to be. "Please?"

"Yes, I'll come. Reed, I didn't mean to make a scene."

"Neither did I. Maddy—" He hesitated a moment, then decided to start clearing the air now. "The business with my father. It had nothing to do with the party he's planning. It had nothing to do with you coming or being with me."

She wanted to believe him, but an insecurity she hadn't been aware of held her back. "What was it, then?"

"I haven't seen him so...charmed by anyone in a very long time. He wanted a house full of children, and he never had them. If he'd had a daughter, I imagine he'd have enjoyed one like you."

"Reed, I'm sorry. I don't know what you want me to do."

"Just don't hurt him. I won't see him hurt again." He touched her cheek briefly, then left her at the stage door.

Chapter Seven

When Maddy let herself into her apartment she was thinking about Reed. That didn't surprise her. Thoughts of Reed had dominated her day to the point where she had had to make a conscious effort to concentrate on her role as Mary Howard. The Philadelphia opening was only three weeks away. She couldn't afford to be distracted by speculation on what-if and how-to when they concerned Reed Valentine.

But what was going to happen on Saturday? What would she say? How should she behave?

Maddy jammed the key into her lock and called herself a fool. But she kept thinking.

The lights were on. As the door closed behind her, Maddy stood in the center of the room frowning. True, she was often absentminded or in too much of a rush to remember little details, but she wouldn't have left the lights on. She'd retained the habit of conserving energy—and electrical bills—from her leaner days. Besides, she didn't think she'd even turned them on that morning before she'd left for class.

Odder still, she could have sworn she smelled coffee. Fresh coffee.

Maddy was setting down her dance bag and turning toward the kitchen when she heard a noise from the bedroom. Heart thudding, she pulled a tap shoe from the bag and held it up like a weapon. She didn't consider herself the aggressive type, but it didn't even occur to her to run and call for help. It was her home, and she had always defended what was hers.

Slowly, careful to make no sound, she moved across the room.

She heard a jangle of hangers from the closet and gripped the shoe tighter. If the thief thought he'd find anything of value in there, he was too stupid for words. She should be able to send a dim-witted thief on his way with the threat of a rap over the head with a reinforced heel. Still, the closer she came, the more often she had to swallow past the little flutter of panic in her throat.

Holding her breath, Maddy closed her free hand around the knob, then pulled. There were simultaneous shrieks of alarm.

"Well." Chantel put **a h**and to her heart. "It's nice to see you, too."

"Chantel!" With a whoop of delight, Maddy tossed her shoe aside and grabbed her sister. "I almost put a dent in your head."

"Then I'd have one to match yours."

"What are you doing here?"

"Hanging up a few things." Chantel kissed Maddy's cheek, then tossed back her silvery-blond mane.

"I hope you don't mind. Silk wrinkles so dreadfully."

"Of course I don't mind. I meant, what are you doing in New York? You should have let me know you were coming."

"Darling, I wrote you last week."

"No, you—" Then Maddy remembered the stack of mail she'd yet to open. "I haven't gotten to some of my mail yet."

"Typical."

"Yeah, I know." She drew her sister back just to look. It was a face she knew as well as her own, but one she never ceased to admire. The subtle French fragrance that wafted through the room suited Chantel as perfectly as the deep blue eyes and the cupid's-bow mouth. "Oh, Chantel, you look wonderful. I'm so glad to see you."

"You look pretty wonderful yourself." Chantel studied her sister's glowing complexion. "Either those vitamins you guzzle are working or you're in love."

"I think it's both."

One thin, shapely brow rose. "Is that so? Why don't we get out of the closet and talk about it?"

"Let's sit down and have a drink." Maddy linked her arm through Chantel's. "Oh, I wish Abby were here, too. Then it would be perfect. How long are you in town?"

"Just a couple of days," Chantel explained as they walked back to the living room. "I'm presenting one of those America's Choice Awards Friday night. My publicists thought it would be 'just nifty'."

Maddy began to search the cupboards for a bottle of wine. "And you don't."

Chantel tossed a glance at the darkening window. "You know New York's not my town, darling. It's too..."

"Real?" Maddy suggested.

"Let's just say noisy." Outside, two sirens were competing in volume. "I hope you have some wine, Maddy. You were out of coffee, you know."

"I gave it up," Maddy told her with her head stuck in a cupboard.

"Gave it up? You?"

"I was drinking too much of it. Just pouring that caffeine into my system. I'm drinking mostly herb tea these days." Maddy sniffed again and caught the rich, dark scent of coffee. "Where did you get it?"

"Oh, I borrowed a few scoops from your next-door neighbor."

Wine bottle in hand, Maddy drew out of the cupboard. "Not Guido."

"Yes, Guido. The one with the biceps and large teeth."

Maddy unearthed two glasses. "Chantel, I've lived next door to him for years and I wouldn't exchange a good-morning with him without an armed guard."

"He was charming." Leaning against the counter, Chantel pushed her hair away from her face. "Although I did have to discourage him from coming over to fix the coffee for me."

Maddy glanced at her sister, at the classic face, the stunning body, the Wedgwood-blue eyes that easily hypnotized men. "I bet." Maddy poured two glasses, then tapped hers against her sister's. "Here's to the O'Hurleys."

"God bless them every one," Chantel murmured, and sipped. After a grimace, she swallowed. "Maddy, you're still buying your wine at the flea market."

"It's not that bad. Let's sit down. Have you heard from Abby?"

"I called her before I left so she'd know I'd be on the same coast. She was refereeing a fight between the boys and sounded blissfully happy."

"Dylan?"

Chantel sank into the sofa, grateful for its stationary comfort after a long, tedious flight. "She said he was nearly finished with the book."

"How does she feel about it?"

"Content. She trusts him completely." Chantel sipped again. There was a trace of cynicism in her voice that she couldn't completely disguise. She had trusted once, too. "Abby seems to have put her life with Rockwell behind her. She tells me Dylan's going to adopt the boys."

"That's great." Maddy felt her eyes fill, and swallowed more wine. "That's really great."

"It's what she's needed. He's what she's needed. Oh, and Abby said she'd gotten a lace tablecloth from Trace as a wedding gift."

"I guess we were all hoping he'd manage to get back for the wedding. Where is he?"

"Brittany, I think. He sent his apologies, as usual."

"Do you ever wonder what he does?"

"I decided to stop wondering in case it was illegal. Are Mom and Pop going to make it to your opening?"

"I hope so. They've got three weeks to work their way to Philly. I guess you won't be able to make it back east."

"I'm sorry." Chantel closed her hand over her sister's. "Filming on *Strangers* was postponed—couple of problems with the location site. I should be starting week after next. You know I'd be here if I could."

"I know. You must be so excited. It's such a wonderful part."

"Yes." A frown moved into her eyes and out again.

"What's wrong?"

Chantel hesitated, on the verge of telling Maddy about the anonymous letters she'd been getting. And the phone calls. She shrugged it off. "I don't know. Nerves, I guess. I've never done a miniseries. It's not really television, it's not a feature film."

"Come on, Chantel. This is Maddy."

"It's nothing." She made up her mind not to discuss what was probably nothing more than a minor annoyance. When she returned to California, the whole thing would probably have blown over. "Just a few loose ends I have to tie up. What I want to talk about is the man you're thinking about." She smiled when Maddy blinked back to full attention. "Come on, Maddy. Tell your big sister everything."

"I'm not sure how much there is to tell." Maddy brought her legs up into a comfortable lotus position. "Do you ever remember Pop talking about knowing Edwin Valentine?"

"Edwin Valentine?" Narrowing her eyes, Chantel searched her memory. One of the reasons for her quick rise as an actress in Hollywood was the fact that she never forgot anything—not lines, not names, not faces. "No, I don't remember the name at all."

"He's Valentine Records." Chantel merely lifted a brow again and waited for Maddy to go on. "It's one of the top labels in the business, maybe *the* top. Anyway, he met Mom and Pop when we were babies. He was just getting started, and they let him sleep on a cot in their hotel room."

"Sounds like them," Chantel said easily. She slipped out of her shoes and slouched, something she would never have done with anyone but family. "What's next?"

"Valentine Records is the backer for the play."

"Interesting." She started to sip, then latched on to her sister's hand. "Maddy, you're not involved with him? He must be Pop's age. Look, I'm not saying that age should be a big factor in a relationship, but when it's my little sister—"

"Hang on." Maddy giggled into her wine. "Didn't I read that you were seeing Count DeVargo of De-Vargo Jewelers? He must be hitting sixty."

"That was different." Chantel muttered. "Euro-pean men are ageless."

"Very good," Maddy decided after a moment. "That was really very good."

"Thanks. In any case, we were nothing more than friends. If you're getting dreamy eyed over a man old enough to be your father—"

"I'm not dreamy eyed," Maddy said. "And it's his son."

"Whose son? Oh." Calmer, Chantel settled back again. "So this Edwin Valentine has a son. Not a dancer?"

"No." She had to smile. "He's taken over the re-cord company. I guess he's a magnate."

"Well." Chantel rolled out the word. "Coming up in the world, aren't we?"

"I don't know what I'm doing." Maddy unlaced her legs and rose. "Most of the time I think I must be crazy. He's gorgeous and successful and conservative. He likes French restaurants.''

"The beast."

Maddy dissolved into laughter. "Oh, Chantel, help."

"Have you slept with him?"

It was like Chantel to get right down to brass tacks. Maddy let out a deep breath and sat again. "No."

"But you've thought about it."

"I can't seem to think of much of anything but him."

Chantel reached for the bottle to fill her glass again. Once you got past the first swallow, the wine was almost palatable. "And how does he feel about you?"

"That's where I hit the brick wall. Chantel, he's kind and considerate and has the capacity for such— well, goodness, I guess. But he has this safety net when it comes to women. One minute he's holding me and I feel as though this is what I've been waiting for all of my life. The next minute he's putting me aside as though we hardly know each other."

"Does he know how you feel?"

"I'm half-afraid he does. I wouldn't dare tell him. He's made it clear he's not interested in what he calls 'the long haul'."

Chantel felt a little twist of alarm. "And you're thinking in terms of the long haul?"

"I could spend my life with him." With eyes abruptly serious, abruptly vulnerable, she stared at her sister. "Chantel, I could make him happy."

"Maddy, these things work two ways." God, how well she knew it. "Can he make you happy?"

"If he'd let me in. If he'd let me in just a little so I could understand why he's so afraid to feel. Chantel, something happened, something devastating, I know it, to make him so untrusting. If I knew what it was I could do something about it. But I'm flying blind.''

Chantel set down her glass and took both of Maddy's hands. ''You really love him?''

''I really love him.''

''He's a very lucky man.''

''You're prejudiced.''

''Damn right. And no matter how aloof he is, I don't think he stands a chance. I mean, look at that face.'' She took Maddy's chin in her hand. ''It says trustworthy, loyal, devoted.''

''You make me sound like a cocker spaniel.''

''Maddy...'' It was so easy to give advice, Chantel thought, so easy to give what she would never take herself. ''Very simply, if you love this guy, the best way to get him to love you back is to be what you are.''

Discouraged, Maddy picked up her wine. She'd throw caution to the winds, she decided, and have another half glass. ''I figured you'd give me some tried-and-true tips in the art of seduction.''

''I just did. For you,'' Chantel added. ''Honey, if I told you some of my secrets, your hair would curl. Besides, you're looking for marriage, right?''

''I guess I am.''

''Then while I don't recommend honesty in most relationships, this is different. If you want this man in your life for better or for worse, then you should be up-front. When are you seeing him again?''

''Not until Saturday.''

Chantel frowned a moment. She'd wanted to get a look at this Valentine character herself, but she'd be on a plane heading west on Saturday. ''Well, it wouldn't hurt for you to have a new outfit.'' She cast a look at

Maddy's sweats. "Something alluring, of course, but something that will suit you."

"Do they make things like that?"

"Leave it to me." Chantel took another quick glance and gauged that she and Maddy still wore the same size. "The only thing I really like about New York is the shopping. Speaking of shopping, did you know you only have three carrots and a jug of juice in your fridge?"

"I was going to get something at the health food shop around the corner."

"Spare me from that. I don't like eating twigs."

"There's a restaurant a block away that serves great spaghetti."

"Terrific. Do I have to change or do you?"

Maddy studied her sister's elegant nubby silk suit while fingering her own sweats. "You do. Did you bring anything with you that doesn't look so Rodeo Drive?"

"I can't bring what I don't have. Keeping up an image that looks glamorous and a little decadent is hard work."

With a quick snort, Maddy rose. "I've got something you can toss on that shouldn't tarnish that image of yours too badly. Besides, no one's going to recognize you down at Franco's."

Chantel smiled slowly as she rose. "What odds do you give me?"

Maddy opened her arms to grab her sister. "Chantel, you're one in a million."

Chantel rested her cheek against her sister's. Things should be as simple, she thought, things should be as easy as they were at this moment. "No, we're three in a million. And I'm so glad to have you."

* * *

When Maddy came home from rehearsal on Saturday, the apartment was empty. She'd had almost three days with Chantel. During the brief visit her sister had charmed the surly Guido, awed the production staff of the play with a brief visit during rehearsal and bought out half the stores on Fifth Avenue.

Maddy missed her already.

If Chantel had been able to stay just one more day...

Sighing, Maddy headed for the shower. It was silly to think she needed moral support just to go talk to Reed. She didn't need a pep talk or a vote of confidence. She was simply going to talk to the man about the meaning of their relationship and where it was going.

Maddy turned on the shower and stood, face into the spray, as the water poured over her. She was going to wash, change, then catch the subway uptown. It wasn't as though it were the first time she would have spent an evening in Reed's apartment. Besides, they needed to talk. There was no use being nervous about something that had to be done.

The play was going well. She could tell him that. She could start things off by telling him how right it was beginning to feel. Everything was coming together. When they left the following week for the last days of intense rehearsal in Philadelphia, it was only going to get better. Would he miss her at all? Would he tell her?

Lecturing herself, Maddy stepped out of the shower and immediately searched through the rubble of her linen closet for her hair drier. Within minutes she'd fluffed her hair dry, teased a bit of height on the top and ruffled the sides to give more volume. She pulled out a pile of makeup and began to experiment with an expert hand.

More than once she'd done her own hair and makeup for the stage. She'd learned early that if she didn't want to be dependent on someone else's time and whims, she had to know how to do for herself. She could, if necessary, have chosen the right paints and pots to turn her into Mary, or Suzanna, or any other part she'd ever played. Tonight she was just Maddy.

Satisfied, she headed into the bedroom. There, spread on the bed, was what Chantel had left behind. Maddy picked up the note first and read the bold, looping writing.

Maddy,

After an exhaustive search and hard thinking, I decided this was for you. Happy birthday next month. Wear it tonight for your Reed. Better yet, wear it for yourself. Forget the first reaction that the color isn't right for you. Trust me. I'll be thinking of you. You know I love you, kid. Break a leg.

Chantel

Catching her bottom lip between her teeth, Maddy looked at Chantel's gift. The slinky silk slacks were a bold, flaming pink. Exactly the sort of color Maddy would avoid with her hair. She gave them a dubious look but reached down to touch. The skinny little camisole top was jade-colored. Together they were precisely the sort of outrageous combination she would have chosen herself. Maddy smiled as she picked the top up by the slender straps. But it was the jacket that she, who chose clothes with a careless eye for color and comfort, cooed over.

It was silk, as well, a bit oversize and as slinky as the slacks. Thousands of beads were sewed on it, creating a kaleidoscope of colors. Each way she turned it, a different pattern emerged. At first glance she would have said it was too sophisticated for her taste, too elegant for her style, but the ever-changing patterns caught both her imagination and her admiration.

"All right," she said aloud. "We're going to go for it."

Why was he nervous? Reed paced his too-quiet apartment for the tenth time. It was ridiculous to feel nervous just because he was going to entertain a woman for the evening. Even if the woman was Maddy. Especially because the woman was Maddy, he corrected.

They'd spent evenings together before. But tonight was different. He switched on the stereo, hoping the flow of music would distract him.

He'd purposely avoided contacting her all week to prove to himself he could live without her. Somewhere around Thursday, he had stopped counting the times he'd picked up the phone and dialed the first few digits of her number, only to hang up.

They were just going to talk, he reminded himself. It was becoming imperative that they outline what they wanted from each other, what the rules were, where the boundaries began. He wanted to make love with her. Needed to make love with her, he corrected, and a curl of desire began with just the thought.

They could be lovers and still keep things companionable. That's what they had to get straight before any more time passed. When she came, they would sit down and talk about their needs and their restrictions like reasonable adults. They would come to a logical understanding and go on from there. No one would be hurt.

He was going to hurt her. Reed ran a hand over the back of his neck and wondered why he was so certain of that. He could still remember the way her eyes had filled the last time he'd seen her. How she'd somehow looked both wounded and courageous.

How many times had he told himself he would use tonight to break it off, to sever it all before it went any farther? How many times had he ultimately admitted it wouldn't be possible?

She was getting under his skin, and he couldn't allow that. The best way, the only way, he knew to stop it was to set down the rules.

He paced again, to the windows and back before looking at his watch. She was late. She was driving him crazy.

What was it about her? he asked himself. She wasn't particularly beautiful. She wasn't smooth and sleek and alluringly cool. In short, she wasn't the sort of woman who caught his notice. She was the woman who'd caught him by the throat. He had to loosen her hold, gain control, go forward at his own pace.

Where the hell was she?

When the knock sounded, he was cursing her. Reed gave himself a moment to settle. It wouldn't do to open the door edgy and eager. If he started on solid ground, he'd stay on solid ground. Then he opened the door, and every logical thought deserted him.

Had he said she wasn't really beautiful? How could he have been so totally wrong? He's said she wasn't

alluring, yet she stood there, glittering, glowing, simmering with her own source of energy, and he'd never
been more captivated.

"Hi. How are you?" He couldn't tell her heart was
thudding uneasily as she smiled and kissed his cheek.

"I'm fine." That was the scent he'd carried with
him for days. It was absurd for a man to linger on
something that could be bought at a department-store
cosmetics counter.

Maddy hesitated a moment. "You did say you
wanted to see me Saturday night, didn't you?"

"Yes."

"Well, are you going to let me in?"

The humor in her eyes made him feel like a fool.
"Of course. Sorry." He closed the door behind her
and wondered if he'd just made the biggest mistake of
his life. And hers. "You look wonderful. Different."

"You think so?" Smiling again, she *pirouetted*.
"My sister breezed into town for a couple of days and
picked this out for me." She turned again, wanting to
share her pleasure. "Great, isn't it?"

"Yes. You're beautiful."

It was easy to pass it off with a laugh. "Well, the
outfit certainly is. You haven't been by rehearsals."

"No." Because he'd needed to give himself time
away from her. "Would you like a drink?"

"A little white wine, maybe." She crossed, as she
invariably did, to his view of the city. "It's really
coming together, Reed. Everything's starting to click."

"The accounting department will be glad to hear
it."

It was his dry tone that made her laugh. "How can
you lose? If we hit, you rake it in. If we flop, you write
it off as a tax break. But it's alive, Reed." She took the

glass from him, needing him to feel it with her. "Every time I walk out into a scene as Mary, it becomes more alive. I need that sort of vibrant, breathing center to my life."

A center to her life. He'd always scrupulously avoided having one in his own. "And a play does that for you?"

She looked down at her wine, then out at the city again. "If I were alone, with nothing more, without a chance for anything more, I could be happy. When I'm onstage... When I'm onstage," she began again, "and I look out and see a theater full of people, waiting for me... Reed, I don't know how to explain it."

"Try." He stood watching her, watching the city lights glow behind her. "I want to know."

She pulled a hand through the hair she'd so carefully styled. It fell back into place, just a little mussed. "I feel instant acceptance. I guess I feel loved. And I can give the love back, with a dance, with a song. It sounds hokey to say that's what I was born for. But it was. It just was."

"It would be enough if you could stand on stage and be loved by hundreds of strangers?"

She gave him a long, searching look, knowing he didn't understand. No one who didn't perform could. "It would be enough, would have to be enough, if that were all I could have."

"You don't need one single permanent person or thing in your life."

"I didn't say that." She kept her eyes on his as she shook her head slowly. "I meant that I've always been able to adjust. I've had to. Applause fills a lot of gaps, Reed. All of them, if you work hard at it. I imagine your work does the same for you."

"It does. I told you before I don't have the time or the inclination for a long-term relationship."

"Yes, you did."

"I meant it, Maddy." He drank again, because the words didn't come comfortably through his lips. Why, when he was trying so hard to be honest, did it feel as though he were lying? "We tried it your way. The friendship."

Her fingers were cold. She set her glass down and linked them together to warm them. "I think it worked."

"I want more." He ran his hand through her hair and brought her closer. "And if I take more, I'm going to hurt you."

That was the truth. She knew it, accepted it, then told herself to forget it. "I'm responsible for myself, Reed. That includes my emotions. I want more, too. Whatever happens, the choice was mine."

"What choice?" he demanded suddenly. "What choice, Maddy? Isn't it time to admit neither of us has had one all along? I wanted to push you aside. That was my choice. But I kept drawing you closer and closer." He had his hands on her shoulders now and slowly slid the jacket from them. It fell to the floor in a waterfall of color. "You don't know me," he murmured as he felt the quick tremble that moved through her body. "You don't know what's inside me. There's a lot there you wouldn't like, more you wouldn't even understand. If you were smart, you'd be out that door now."

"Guess I'm not smart."

"It wouldn't matter." His fingers tensed on her shoulders. "Because I'm past the point of letting you go." Her skin was warm, so warm and soft in his hands. "You'll hate me before it's finished." And he already regretted it.

"I don't hate easily. Reed . . ." Wanting to soothe, she lifted a hand to his cheek. "Trust me a little."

"Trust has nothing to do with this." Something flared in his eyes, quickly, vibrantly, then was gone. "Not a damn thing. I want you, and that hunger's been clawing inside me for weeks. That's all I have for you."

The hurt came, as promised, but she pushed it aside. "If that were true, I don't think you would have been fighting it so hard."

"I've finished fighting it." His lips descended upon hers. "You'll stay with me tonight."

"Yes, I'll stay." She put both hands to his face, wanting to ease the tension in him. "Because it's what I want."

He took her wrists, then slowly slid her hand through his until he could press his lips to her palm. It was a promise, the only one he could give her. "Come with me."

Leading with her heart, Maddy went.

Chapter Eight

There was a lamp in the hall that sent a shaft of light into the bedroom. Otherwise all was shadows and secrets. He'd left the stereo on, but it was hardly more than an echo of a sound now as they stopped to touch each other.

She'd wanted to see his eyes like this, intensely focused only on her and what he wanted from her. It made her smile as she yielded her lips to his again.

"You're making a mistake," he began.

"Shhh." She moved her lips over his. "Let's be logical later. I've wanted to know what it would be like with you from the moment I met you." Watching his face, she began to unbutton his shirt. "I've wanted to know what you looked like. What you felt like." She drew his shirt off, then ran her hands up his chest. It was hard, smooth and, at the moment, stiff. "I'd lie awake at night wondering when we'd be together like this.'' Seeking, curious, her hands stroked his shoulders, then moved slowly down his arms. "Reed, I'm not afraid of you, or of how I feel.''

"You should be.''

Her head tilted back. Her eyes challenged. "Then show me why.''

With an oath he gave in to her, to himself, to everything. Dragging her against him, he crushed her mouth beneath his and plundered. He ran his hands all over the thin silk that covered her, until her body began to shiver. Was it fear or anticipation? He couldn't tell. But her fingers dug into his flesh, holding him close, and her mouth was open and eager.

He'd once wondered if she were a witch. The thought returned now, as what rose between them was all hellsmoke and temptation. There was nothing easy about her now, nothing light and simple. The passion that swirled around him seemed as complex and dangerous as Eve or the serpent who had dared her.

Desire clawed at him, fierce and heartless. He wanted to take her quickly, instantly, where they stood, living only for the moment, no strings, no promises. It would be better for her, better for him, if he did.

Then she murmured his name with a sound as soft and sweet as an evening breeze.

His hands gentled. He couldn't resist it. His mouth softened. He couldn't prevent it. There would come a time when he would hurt her. But tonight was special. He thought of nothing but her, not the past, not the future. Tonight he would give as much as he could, take as much as he dared. And perhaps he could give to himself, as well.

Gently he brushed the straps from her shoulders, and the brilliant silk slithered down to cling tentatively to her breasts. As if she sensed his change of mood, she went very still. Was she so willing to absorb his moods? He hoped for her sake she had some defenses left.

With a tenderness that surprised him more than it did her, he skimmed his lips over her bare shoulders, taking in the texture, as smooth as the silk, and her scent, just as tantalizing. She suddenly seemed so small, so fragile, so young. After a moment's hesitation, he brought his lips back to merge with hers.

She felt the change in him. The tug-of-war that always seemed to rage inside him seemed to cease. Her own open heart was ready to take him in.

She stroked carefully, pleased with the long, hard lines of his body. Though her breathing was no longer steady, she allowed her lips to nibble and tease only, to give him time to accept what was happening between them. He would fight it. She was nearly certain he would deny it, but his feelings were guiding him. Willing, pliant, they both moved to the bed.

She knew her body too well to feel awkward. Her hips were narrow, her legs long, her torso just a shade too thin. She was built like a dancer and didn't question it, just as she didn't question his cautious, careful exploration.

The camisole slipped off and was tossed aside. When his hands touched her skin, she merely sighed and let sensation rule. With her eyes half closed, she could see the dark, bronzed sweep of his hair as it brushed over her. She could feel her heart racing, pounding. Then his tongue traced over her nipple and her body contracted with a new, dizzying surge of pleasure.

She moved with him, as though the choreography between them had been long since plotted. Action and reaction, move and countermove. For Maddy it was as effortless and natural as breathing.

Wherever his desire took him, wherever his needs led, she was waiting, willing. He'd never experienced anything, anyone, like her. Her body sizzled with heat. He could feel the pulses throb wherever he touched, whenever he tasted. He'd never known anyone so open to loving, so free and uninhibited. When she unhooked his slacks and drew them down, her touch on his flesh was honest, generous, as though they'd known, touched and taken from each other since time began.

His own pulse was raging. She found it in the crook of his elbow and murmured as she pressed her lips against it. When he was naked, she looked at him with frank appreciation. With an easy smile, a gentle laugh, she gathered him close, embracing him with both passion and affection. A shudder rippled through him, leaving him dazed, confused and aching for her.

"Kiss me again," she murmured. When he looked, he saw her eyes half closed, with that tawny, feline look that shaded them so unexpectedly. "I love what happens to me when I'm kissing you."

She brought his face close and let herself be swept away.

"I've wanted you to touch me," she said against his lips. "Sometimes I'd imagine what it would be like to have your hands on me. Here." Nearly purring, she guided his hand. "And here. I can't get enough." She arched under him like a bow. "I don't think I'll ever get enough."

Something was slipping away from him—the control he kept tightly locked on his emotions. He couldn't afford to give her his heart, couldn't trust her with the power that went with the gift. Instead, he could give her the passion she sought and accepted so beautifully.

He pulled the silk pants off her, watching as they glided erotically over her flesh. The wisp that she wore beneath slid down and was discarded. Suddenly, so suddenly he couldn't mark the change, he was beyond being sensible, beyond being reasonable. Desire for her, for everything she was, everything she offered, clawed through his system. Perhaps this wasn't the kind of passion he'd been prepared for, but it raged through him, too strong and real to be harnessed. With her honesty and her zest for life, she'd begun this journey. He wouldn't be merely a passenger; here they would meet one to one. He would finally set free the needs she'd aroused in him from the first.

He forgot gentleness, so that when his mouth crushed hers it was with rough desperation. His hands, always so careful, raced over her until she was writhing and murmuring mindlessly beneath him. With each movement, each sigh, his heart thudded faster, pounding in his brain in a beat that somehow sounded like her name. Without hesitation she wrapped around him, and he took her. He heard a moan low in her throat before his own breath caught.

She was so warm, so unbelievably soft and welcoming. He struggled to regain that edge of control as her body began to move, graceful as a waltz, erotic as any primitive rite. He moved above her, wanting to see what the feel of him did to her. Pleasure shuddered over her face, but her eyes stayed open and on his.

She trembled, and the bedspread slithered through her fingers as she gripped it. Such power, such strength. Nothing she'd ever experienced could match it. If she'd left the world she'd known, she felt no need to return to it. Here, she could remain here, while centuries flew by.

Then they were tangled tightly as the storm plucked them both up and threw them together. Her body tensed, shivering on the edge before the release came in floods of unspeakable pleasure.

She would take the moon and the stars he offered. Maddy wrapped her arms around him and knew she would wait until he offered himself, as well.

She was gone when he woke up. Reed felt the loss swiftly, sharply, when he turned toward where she'd slept and found the bed beside him empty. From the living room, the stereo that had never been switched off droned out the Sunday-morning news as he lay back and explored the feeling of emptiness.

Why should he feel empty? He'd spent an exciting night with an exciting woman, and now she'd gone on her way. That was what he'd wanted. That was the way the game was played. Throughout the night they had given each other comfort, warmth and passion. Now the sun was up and it was over. He should be grateful she took it all so casually that she could slip out the door without even a goodbye.

Why should he feel empty? He couldn't afford to regret that she wasn't there to give him a sleepy smile and snuggle against him. He was the one who knew how transient and shallow relationships really were. He should admire her for being honest enough to acknowledge that what had passed between them during the night had been nothing more than mutual physical release. There had been no pledges given, no pledges asked for, just a few hours of mindless pleasure that required no excuses or explanations.

Why should he feel so empty?

Because she was gone, and he wanted to hold her.

Swearing, Reed pushed himself up in bed. As he raked a hand through his hair, he spotted a pool of pink silk on the floor beside the bed.

But she was gone. Reed tossed aside the sheet and got out of bed to pick up the slacks he'd drawn slowly down Maddy's legs the night before. Even Maddy couldn't get far without them. He was still holding them when he heard his front door open. Reed tossed the slacks over the back of the chair beside the bed, then reached for a robe.

He found her in the kitchen, setting a brown grocery bag on the counter.

"Maddy?"

She let out a muffled squeal and jumped back. "Reed!" With a hand to her heart, she closed her eyes a moment. "You scared me to death. I thought you were sleeping."

And he'd thought she was gone. Cautious, he held himself back. "What are you doing?"

"I went out to get breakfast."

He didn't feel empty any longer. But even as the pleasure came, so did the wariness. "I thought you'd left."

"Don't be silly. I wouldn't just leave." She combed her fingers through hair that hadn't yet seen a brush that morning. "Why don't you get back in bed? I'll have this put together in a minute."

"Maddy..." He took a step forward. Then his gaze slid slowly down her body. "What are you wearing?"

"Like it?" Laughing, she caught the hem of his shirt in her fingers and twirled around. "You have excellent taste, Reed. I was very fashionable."

His shirt hung loose over her shoulders, skimmed her thighs and made her look ridiculously attractive. "Is that one of my ties?"

She pressed her lips together to hold back a chuckle as she toyed with the thin black silk she'd used to secure the shirt at the waist. "It was all I could find. Don't worry, I can have it pressed."

Her legs were long and smooth and bare. He looked at them again and shook his head. "You went out like that?"

"Nobody looked twice," she assured him, so easily he thought she probably believed it. "Look, I'm starving." She wrapped her arms around his neck and kissed him with an easy affection that had his pulse thudding. "Get back in bed and I'll bring this in in a minute."

Because he needed a minute to adjust, he obliged her. She wasn't gone, Reed thought as he sat back against the pillows. She was here, in his kitchen, fixing breakfast as though it were the most natural thing in the world. It pleased him. It worried him. He wondered what he was going to do about her.

"I've got extra whipped cream if we need it," Maddy said as she walked in with a tray.

Reed stared at the breakfast she'd fixed as she scooted onto the bed and set the tray between them. "What is that?"

"Sundaes," she told him, dipping a forefinger into a mound of whipped cream. As she laid it on her tongue, she let out a luxurious sigh of pleasure. "Strawberry sundaes."

"Strawberry sundaes," he repeated. "For breakfast? Is this the same Maddy O'Hurley who worries constantly about nutrition and calories?"

"Ice cream's a dairy product," she reminded him as she offered a spoon. "The berries are fresh. What more do you need?"

"Bacon and eggs?"

"Much too much fat and cholesterol—especially since it doesn't taste this good. Anyway, I'm celebrating." She dipped into her bowl.

"Celebrating what?"

Their eyes met quickly and held. Then she seemed to sigh. How could he not know? And because he didn't, how could she explain? "You look wonderful. I feel wonderful. It's Sunday and the sun's shining. That should be enough." Maddy plucked a strawberry out of his bowl and offered it to him. "Go ahead. Live dangerously."

He closed his lips over the berry, drawing the tips of her fingers into his mouth briefly. "And I thought you subsisted on alfalfa sprouts and wheat germ."

"I do most of the time. That's why this is so great." She let the ice cream rest cool on her tongue and closed her eyes. "Usually I jog on Sunday mornings."

Reed sampled the ice cream himself. "Jog?"

"Only three or four miles," she said with a shrug. "Only."

She licked the back of her spoon clean. "But today I'm being decadent."

He skimmed a hand along her knee. "Are you?"

"Absolutely. I'll pay for it tomorrow, so it has to be good."

"Did you plan to stay here and be decadent?"

"Unless you'd rather I go."

He linked his fingers with hers in an uncomplicated gesture that would have surprised him if he'd realized he'd done it. "No, I don't want you to go."

The smile lighted her face. "I can be very decadent."

"I'm counting on it."

Maddy swirled her finger through the whipped cream, then slowly, very slowly, licked it off. "You might be shocked." When she dipped again, Reed took her wrist, then brought the cream and her finger to his own mouth.

"You think so?" He felt her pulse jump as he sucked lightly on her fingertips. "Why don't we see?" Picking up the tray, he set it beside the bed. Her eyes were huge, her body aching, when he looked at her again. "I wondered how you'd look in the morning."

Tilting her head, she lifted a brow. "How do I look?"

"Fresh." With the lightest of touches he stroked her cheek. "Just a bit mussed. Appetizing."

She caught her tongue between her teeth. "I think I like the appetizing best."

"You know, Maddy, you never asked if you could borrow my shirt."

Humor danced in her eyes again, but she answered very seriously. "No, I didn't, did I? That was rude."

"I want it back." He hooked his fingers in the neck of the shirt and drew her closer. "Now."

"Now?" Fast and hot, anticipation rippled through her. "I suppose you want the tie, as well."

"I certainly do."

"I guess you're entitled," she murmured. Kneeling, she loosened the knot, slipped the silk off and handed it to him. She reached for the buttons, hesitated, then began to unfasten them. Her gaze stayed steady on his as the shirt fell open to reveal a thin panel of flesh. Then she smiled as she let the material slide from her shoulders. Without any self-consciousness she stayed as she was while he looked his fill, then took the shirt by the collar and held it out, kneeling in the center of the bed with sunlight streaming over her skin.

"This is yours, I believe."

He brushed the shirt aside, rising on his knees to cup her shoulders in his hands. "I'm becoming fonder of what's inside." He nipped at her chin as his hands slid down over her. "You have the most incredible body. Hard, soft, compact, limber." Compelled, he drew away just to look at her. "I wonder if— Maddy, what's that you're wearing?"

"What?" A little dazed, she followed his gaze downward. "Oh, that's a G-string, of course. Haven't you ever seen one?"

His eyes came back to hers, amused and intrigued. "As a matter of fact, yes. One wonders if you aren't taking your role of the Merry Widow a bit too seriously."

"You didn't say that while I was stripping for you," she pointed out, then linked her hands behind his neck. "I discovered G-strings when I was researching for the part."

"Researching?" He started to kiss her, then drew back again. "Exactly what does that mean?"

"Just what it sounds like. I couldn't go into a role like this without doing some research."

"You went to strip joints." Caught between fury and frustration, he took her chin firmly. "Are you crazy? Do you know what can happen in places like that?"

"Have you had a lot of experience?"

"Yes— No. Damn it, Maddy, don't change the subject."

"I didn't think I was." She smiled at him again. "Reed, I had to get inside Mary a bit. I figured the best way to do it was to talk to some strippers. I met some fascinating people. There was one called Lotta Oomph."

"Lotta—"

"Oomph," Maddy finished. "Her gimmick was poodles. See, she had five poodles, and—"

"I don't think I want to hear it." Though he wanted badly to laugh, he held her firmly. "Maddy, you've no business going into that kind of place."

"Don't be silly. I worked in places not much different than that when I was twelve. It's all fantasy, Reed. For the most part, all you have are people trying to make a living. And talking with some of the women really helped me understand Mary better."

"Mary is a fantasy," he corrected. "What goes on in those places, what can go on in those places, is hard reality."

"I understand reality very well, Reed." She lifted a hand to his cheek, touched that he would be concerned. "I'm not saying stripping's an admirable profession, or that every stripper's another Gypsy Rose Lee, but most of the people I talked with took a great deal of pride in their act."

"I don't intend to argue the morals or the social significance of exotic dancing, Maddy. I just don't like the idea of you going into one of those joints downtown."

"Well, I don't intend to make a habit of it." She lowered her lashes, trailing a finger down his chest. "I wouldn't mind seeing the poodles again."

"Maddy."

The lashes came up, revealing laughter. "They were pretty amazing."

"So are you." He ran a hand over her hip where the thin string rested. "And what's the story on this?"

"Comfort." She began to nibble quietly on his earlobe. "Every woman in America should wear a G-string."

"You always wear one?" He spread his hand over her, feeling soft skin, firm muscle.

"Mmm. Under street clothes."

"That day we went to see the exhibition of Victorian architecture. You had on those baggy khaki slacks that looked like army surplus."

"They are army surplus."

"You had one of these on underneath?"

"Mm-hmmm."

"Do you know what might have happened if I'd known?"

Content, she rubbed her cheek against his. "What?"

"Right there in front of the model of Queen Victoria's summer home?"

The giggle bubbled out as he scooped her up. "What?"

"With the family of four from New Jersey right behind us?"

"Oh, God." She wrapped her arms around him. "Maybe we can go back this afternoon."

"Not a chance." He buried his face in her throat.

He wasn't supposed to feel like laughing when he had a naked woman beneath him. Lovemaking was a serious business, to be respected and treated with caution and care. He wasn't supposed to feel like a teenager romping in a back seat on a darkened road. He was a grown man, experienced, aware.

But when he rolled over on the bed with her, the laughter was there. It was there when he held her hard against him, when she snuggled into him, when he touched, when she offered. His delight in her was so great, so immense, that laughter seemed the only answer. She accepted it so beautifully, answering with laughter of her own. Even later, not so very much later, when laughter turned to sighs, the joy wasn't dimmed.

There was so much love in her. Maddy wondered that it didn't burst out and light up the room. Every moment she was with him, he grew just a little brighter. Every time he looked at her, his eyes seemed to shimmer.

He was so kind, so gentle, so thorough. So desperate with need for her. If she hadn't already given him her heart, she would have done so then just as freely.

How could she have known there was so much to discover? So much pleasure, so many sensations. She'd never shown that much generosity to another, but with Reed, it was easy.

She knew her body intimately, its strengths, its weaknesses. How strange it was to discover she had known so little about its needs. When his mouth closed over her breast, she felt incredible sensations tighten inside her: pleasure, pain, desperation. A stroke of his hand down her thigh made her shudder. A brush of his lips at her throat made her moan. The body she disciplined so religiously became a morass of needs, of confusion, of anticipation, when he pressed against her.

Touching him made her weak. He was only flesh, blood, bone, but stroking her hands over him made her spirit soar. He was hers. She told herself it didn't matter that it was only for the moment. It didn't matter that it was only pretend. He was hers as long as they were flesh to flesh, mouth to mouth.

He needed her. She could feel the rush of excitement move through him. If, even for one brief moment, he untied the bonds on his emotions, he could love her. She was sure of it. There was more than passion when he held her, more than heat and lust. There was caring and compassion. When his lips brushed over hers, when he allowed the kiss to deepen slowly until they were both swimming in it, she knew that he was on the edge of giving her what she wanted so badly to give him.

Love. It healed, it soothed, it protected. She wanted to tell him how wonderful it was to feel so irrevocably bound to another. She wanted to offer him a glimpse of what it was to know there was someone there for him, someone who would always be there.

His skin was hot and damp. His hands lost their gentleness degree by degree as her excitement grew. She was wild, hungry, avid. Her energy seemed boundless and pushed him farther and farther, to the borders of his control.

The stereo blared on. Outside, the heat rose in waves. It didn't matter. Nothing mattered but them and what they could give each other.

She rolled over him, arms and legs snaking out to hold him close. Agile and desperate, she arched to take him into her. When their sanity shattered, then re-formed, they were still together.

Limp, drained, glowing, Maddy lowered herself to him. Her skin was damp and seemed to fuse naturally with his. She could hear his heartbeat through the dull buzzing in her head. When his hand came to stroke her back, she closed her eyes and surrendered everything.

"Oh, Reed, I love you."

At first she was too caught up in her own dream to feel the stiffening of his body beneath hers. She was too giddy to notice the quick tensing of his fingers on her back. But gradually her mind cleared. Maddy kept her eyes closed a moment longer, knowing that now the words had been said they couldn't be taken back.

"I'm sorry." She took a last long breath and looked up. His expression was shuttered. Though they were still tangled together, he'd distanced himself. "I'm not sorry I said it, or that I feel it, I'm sorry you don't want it."

He told himself that the rush of feeling was regret, not hope. "Maddy, I don't believe in catchphrases, or the need for them."

"Catchphrases." She shook her head as if to clear it. "You consider 'I love you' a catchphrase?"

"What else?" Taking her by the shoulders, he shifted them both until they were sitting. "Maddy, we have something good between us. Let's not cover it with comfortable lies."

What she swallowed wasn't bitterness but hurt. "I don't lie, Reed."

Something moved inside him, something warm. He didn't quite recognize it as another surge of hope before he forced it back. "Fantasize, then."

Her voice was quiet, not quite steady, when she spoke again. "You don't believe I could love you?"

"Love's just a word." He rolled out of bed, grabbing his robe again. "It exists, certainly. Father to son, mother to daughter, brother to sister. When it comes to a man and woman, there are things like attraction, infatuation, even obsession. They come and go, Maddy."

She could only stay where she was and stare at him. "You don't really believe that."

"I know it." He cut her off so sharply she flinched. He regretted his harshness instantly, but he swallowed the regret. "People come together because they want something from each other. They stay together until they want something from someone else. While they're together they make promises they don't intend to keep and say things they don't mean. Because it's expected. I have no expectations."

Suddenly cold, she drew the sheet up. To Reed, she looked terribly young and small and vulnerable. "I've never told another man that I loved him. I don't suppose that matters."

He couldn't let it. There was no way to explain it to her. "I don't want the words, Maddy." He walked to the window, his back to her. Why should he hurt? he wondered. He was only speaking the truth. "I can't give them back to you."

"Why, I wonder." Determined not to cry, she pressed the heels of her hands against her eyes for a moment. "What was it that happened to lock off your emotions, Reed? What's made you so hell-bent to stay untouched? I said I loved you." Her voice rose as she allowed the fury to overwhelm the pain. "I'm not ashamed of it. I didn't say it to pull some sort of declaration from you. It's simply the truth. You're looking for lies where there aren't any."

She wouldn't lose her temper, she told herself as she drew breath in and out slowly. But she wasn't finished. They weren't finished. "Are you going to try to tell me you didn't *feel* anything just now? Do you really believe we had sex and nothing more?"

When he turned, his struggle was all internal. Nothing showed on his face. "I don't have anything more to give you. Take it or leave it, Maddy."

Her fingers tightened on the sheet, but she nodded. "I see."

"I need some coffee." He turned on his heel and left her alone. His hands were shaking. Why did he feel as though everything he'd said had been someone else's thoughts, someone else's words?

What was wrong with him? Reed slammed the kettle on the burner, then leaned both palms on the counter. When she'd said she loved him, part of him had wanted and needed it. Part of him had believed it.

He was becoming a fool over her. That had to stop. He had a prime example of what happens to a man who trusts a woman, who devotes his life to her. Reed had promised himself he wouldn't allow himself the same vulnerability. Maddy couldn't change that. He couldn't let her.

She might actually believe she loved him. It wouldn't take long for her to realize differently. In the meantime, they simply had to go on carefully and play by the rules.

He heard the front door open, then close again. For a long time, Reed simply stood there. Even when the water began to steam and boil, he only stood there. He knew she was gone this time. And he felt hideously empty.

Chapter Nine

I don't care if you've scheduled open-heart surgery, you are going to that party tonight."

Maddy pulled on a high-top sneaker. "Wanda, what's the big deal?"

"No big deal." Wanda pulled Maddy's eye-covered sweatshirt over her head, then studied the results. "You're going to go home and put on your fancy dress and party."

"I just said I was a little tired and not in the mood for a party."

"And I say you're sulking."

"Sulking?" Eyes narrowed, Maddy pulled on her second shoe. She was ready for a fight, primed for it. "I don't sulk."

Wanda plopped down beside her on the bench. "You're an expert at sulking."

"Don't push it, Wanda. I'm in a very mean mood."

Wanda seriously doubted that Maddy could be mean if she took a course in it. "Look, if you don't want to talk about what a jerk your guy is, fine."

"He's not my guy."

"Who's not your guy?"

Frustration came out in a low whistle under her breath. "*He.* He is not my guy. I do not have a guy, I do not want a guy. Therefore, whoever *he* is, he can't be mine."

"Uh-huh." Wanda examined her nails and decided that particular shade of red was very becoming. "But he is a jerk."

"I didn't say—" Her humor got the better of her, and she grinned. "Yeah, he's a jerk."

"Honey, they all are. The point is, Mr. Valentine senior's throwing us this bash, and the star of the show can't go home and pout in her bathtub."

"I wasn't going to." Maddy tied an elaborate bow with her laces. "I was going to pout in bed."

Wanda watched Maddy tie her other shoe. "If you don't go, I'm going to tell everyone in the company that you think you're too classy to party with us."

Maddy snorted. "Who'd believe you?"

"Everybody. 'Cause you won't be there."

Maddy lunged off the bench and began to drag a brush through her hair. "Look, why don't you lay off?"

"Because I like your face."

Wanda only grinned when Maddy scowled at her. "I'm just too tired to go, that's all."

"Bull. I've been rehearsing with you for weeks now. You don't get tired."

Maddy let the brush clatter into the sink. In the reflection, her eyes met Wanda's. "I'm tired tonight."

"You're sulking tonight."

"I'm not—" Yes, she was, she admitted silently. "He'll be there," she blurted out. "I don't— I just don't think I can handle it."

The saucy look was replaced by concern. Wanda rose to drape an arm around Maddy's shoulder. "Hit hard?"

"Yeah." Maddy pressed her fingers between her eyes. "Real hard."

"Had a good cry yet?"

"No." She shook her head, fighting for composure. "I didn't want to be any more of a fool than I already was."

"You're a fool if you don't cry it out." Wanda tugged her back to the bench. "Sit down here and put your head on Wanda's shoulder."

"I didn't think it would hurt so bad," Maddy managed as the tears started to fall.

"Who does?" Keeping her voice quiet, Wanda patted her arm. "If we knew how bad it can be, we wouldn't come within ten feet of a man. But we keep going back, because sometimes it's the best there is."

"It stinks."

"To high heaven."

"He's not worth crying over." She wiped the back of her hand over her cheek.

"Not one of them is. Except, of course, the right one."

"I love him, Wanda."

Wanda carefully drew back far enough to study Maddy's face. "The real thing?"

"Yeah." She didn't bother to wipe the tears away again. "Only he doesn't love me back. He doesn't even want me to love him. Somehow I always thought when I got hit the other person would get hit, too, and we'd go on to happy-ever-after. Reed doesn't even think love exists.''

''That's his problem.''

''No, it's mine, too, because I've been trying for days and days to get over him and I can't.'' She drew in a deep breath. There would be no more tears. ''So you see why I can't go tonight.''

''Hell, no. I see why you have to go.''

''Wanda—''

''Look, honey, go home and bury your head in the sand and you're going to feel the same way tomorrow.'' When she spoke again, there was a toughness in her voice that made Maddy's spine straighten. ''What do you do when an audience freezes up on you and sits there like a bunch of mummies?''

''I want to go stomp off to my dressing room.''

''But what do you do?''

Maddy sighed and brushed her hands over her damp face. ''I stand onstage and sweat it out.''

''And that's what you have to do tonight. And if I'm any judge of men, he's going to be doing some sweating of his own. I saw the way he watched you when he and his old man came to rehearsal. Come on, let's get started. We've got to get dressed.''

Maddy revved herself up to see Reed again the same way she revved herself up to face an audience. She told herself she knew her lines, she knew her moves, and if she made a mistake she'd cover it before anyone noticed. She chose a strapless dress that hugged her hips and draped sensuously down her body and was slit up the side to the middle of her thigh. If she was going to flop, she was going to look great doing it.

Still, as she stood in front of Edwin Valentine's imposing front door, she had to talk herself out of turning around and running for cover.

Setting her chin, she knocked. She was prepared to face him again. She was prepared to act casual and cool. The one thing she wasn't prepared for was the possibility that Reed would open the door himself. She stared at him, astonished at how much emotion could churn inside the human body.

He wondered why his fingers hadn't simply crushed the faceted glass knob he gripped as he looked at her.

"Hello, Maddy."

"Reed." She wouldn't smile. It simply wasn't possible just yet. But she wouldn't collapse at his feet, either. "I hope I'm not early."

"No. As a matter of fact, my father's been waiting for you."

"Then I'll go say hello right away." The blare of a trumpet pealed out from down the hall. "I take it the party's down there." She skirted around him, ignoring the knot in her stomach.

"Maddy."

Bracing herself, she looked carelessly over her shoulder. "Yes?"

"Are you . . . how have you been?"

"Busy." The bell rang behind him, and she lifted a brow. "It looks like you've got your hands full, too. See you later." She walked blindly down the hall, blinking furiously to clear her vision.

The party was in full swing. Maddy stepped into it and allowed herself to be caught up in the good feelings, the excitement and the camaraderie. She exchanged a few quick, careless embraces and fended of a more intimate one from a member of the brass section.

"I was beginning to think you'd backed out." Wanda, who'd been talking to one of the musicians, came up beside her, a jerk of her head sending the horn player on his way.

"Nope. Nobody can call an O'Hurley a coward."

"Might help you to know that the younger Valentine has been watching the door for the last half hour."

"He has?" She started to turn around, to look for him, then stopped herself. "No, it doesn't matter. Let's have a drink. Champagne?"

"Yeah, Mr. Valentine's a real sport. You know, he's a nice man." Wanda took a glass of champagne and downed it in one shot. "Not stuffy. He acts as though we're real people."

"We are real people."

"Don't spread that around." A slow gleam came into Wanda's eyes as she looked over Maddy's shoulder. "There's Phil. I've decided to let him convince me he has serious intentions. Not necessarily *honorable*," she added as her smile widened. "Just serious."

"Phil?" Interested, Maddy eyed the dancer who played Wanda's partner. "Well, does he?"

"Maybe, maybe not." Wanda grabbed another glass of champagne. "The fun's in finding out."

Wishing she could agree, Maddy turned to the buffet table where groups of hungry dancers crowded together. Eat, drink and be merry, she told herself. For tomorrow we go to Philadelphia.

"Maddy."

Before she could choose between the pâté and the quiche, Edwin came up behind her.

"Oh, Mr. Valentine. What a great party."

"Edwin," he corrected, as he took her hand and kissed it in a courtly gesture that made her smile. "It has to be Edwin if you're going to give me the dance you promised."

"Then it's Edwin, and it will be my pleasure." With a hand on his shoulder, she moved into step with him. "I got in touch with my parents," she began. "They're in New Orleans, but they're going to make it for opening night in Philly. I was hoping you'd be there."

"Wouldn't miss it. You know, Maddy, this play is the best thing I've done for myself in years. I thought it was time I let myself grow old, you know."

"That's the most ridiculous thing I've ever heard."

"You're so young." He patted the back of her waist where his hand guided her. "When you come up on sixty, you look around and say to yourself, okay, it's time to slow down now. You've earned it. You should relax and enjoy your waning years."

"Waning years." She tossed her hair back and grinned at him. "Phooey."

"Well, that's about it." He chuckled down at her, and she wondered why Reed hadn't inherited those kind, dark eyes. "After I'd retired, I realized I wanted a bit more than eighteen holes every Wednesday. I needed youth around me, their vitality. Reed's always kept me young, you know. As much my best friend as my son. A man couldn't do any better."

"He loves you very much."

Something in her tone had him glancing down. "Yes, he does. I wanted to give him a chance with the business without me hanging around, poking into things. He's done well. More than well," he said with a sigh. "Reed's put his whole life into the business. Maybe that's a mistake."

"He doesn't think so."

"No? I wonder. Well, in any case, until this play came along I didn't know what the hell I was going to do with myself. Now I think I found out."

"Broadway fever?"

"Exactly." Somehow he'd known she would understand him. He could only hope she would understand his son, as well. "Once this play's established, I'm going to hunt myself up another. I figure I've got myself an expert whose opinion I can ask for and trust."

She saw the question in his eyes and nodded slowly. "If you want to play angel, Edwin, I'll be glad to play devil's advocate."

"I knew I could count on you. I've been around entertainers all my life, Maddy. Made my living off them. That kind of punch just can't be replaced with a golf ball." He gave her a quick, companionable pat. "Let's get you something to eat."

A glance at the buffet table had her sighing. "My hero."

The music changed from mellow to manic as three members of the cast jumped together to belt out a medley of Broadway hits. It didn't take long for Phil to pull Wanda stage center for an impassioned *pas de deux*. The chorus of cheers turned quickly into a challenge of champions as another couple swirled out.

"Come on, Maddy," Terry said, taking her by the hand. "We can't let them show us up."

"Sure we can," Maddy told him, and reached for the pâté again.

"No. We've got a reputation to uphold. Remember the number from *Within Reach*?"

"That was the biggest bomb I ever rode into the ground."

"So the play stunk," he said easily. "But the dances we had together were terrific. We got the only good reviews. Come on, Maddy, for old time's sake."

He tugged on her arm and grinned. Unable to resist, Maddy went into a series of pirouettes that ended with them caught close. The few dancers who recognized the moves went into a round of applause.

It was a slow, seductive number with long moves and extended holds that took perfect timing and muscle control. The routine came back to her, as though she'd rehearsed it that afternoon, rather than four years before. The file simply clicked open, and her body remembered.

She felt Terry brace for the lift and *plié* to help him. With the trust of dancer for dancer, she arched back until her hair nearly swept the rug.

Then she was laughing and bouncing back into his arms from the sheer fun of it. "Maybe it wasn't such a bomb," she said breathlessly.

"Baby, it was atomic." Then he gave her a friendly pat on the rump as the music changed tempo and other dancers merged together.

Reed was watching her. When her gaze was drawn to his, Maddy felt the heat rise to her skin along with wishes and regrets. Thinking only of escape, she turned and went through the doors onto the terrace.

The air was hot and sultry there, as if it bounced off the pavement and rose up. Maddy leaned on the banister and gave in to it. She absorbed the noise, the movement and the life of the city beneath her. She could need, she could wish, but she wouldn't regret. Steadying herself, Maddy drew on the strength she'd been born with. She wouldn't regret.

She knew Reed had stepped onto the terrace behind her before he spoke. It had been wrong of her to think of running, to think of hiding in her apartment. He was still what she wanted, like it or not.

"Tell me if you'd rather I go."

It was so like him, she thought, to lay the choices out front. She turned and let herself look at him. "No, of course not."

He curled his hands into his pockets. "Are you generous with everyone, Maddy, or most particularly with me?"

"I don't know. I've never thought about it."

He walked over to the railing, wanting to be just a bit closer. "I've missed seeing you."

"I'd hoped you would." The stars were out and the moon was full. She had that to hold on to, at least. "I was going to come here tonight and be very cool, very breezy. I don't seem to be able to carry it off."

"I watched you dance with my father, and you know what occurred to me?" When she shook her head, he reached out, compelled to touch her, even just a wisp of her hair. "You've never danced with me."

She turned just enough to study his profile. "You've never asked me."

"I'm asking now." He held out his hand, again leaving the choice up to her. She set hers in it without a second thought. They moved together until they were one shadow on the terrace floor. "When you left last week, I thought it was for the best."

"So did I."

He brushed his cheek over her hair. "There hasn't been a day that I haven't thought of you. There hasn't been a day that I haven't wanted you." Slowly, when he felt no resistance, he lowered his mouth to hers. Her lips were as warm and welcoming as always. Her body fit to his as though fate had fashioned her for him, or him for her. The longings that raced through him brought on a panic he rigidly fought down. "Maddy, I want you to come back."

"I want that, too." She lifted her hands to his cheeks. "But I can't."

He gripped her wrists as panic grew. "Why?"

"Because I can't keep to your terms, Reed. I can't stop myself from loving you, and you won't let yourself love me."

"Damn it, Maddy, you're asking for more than I can give."

"No." She stepped a little closer, and her eyes were bright and direct. "No, I'd never ask for more than you were capable of giving, any more than I can give you any less. I love you, Reed. If I came back, I couldn't stop telling you. You couldn't stop backing away from it."

"I want you in my life." Desperation made his hands tense on her. "Isn't that enough?"

"I wish I knew. I want to be part of your life. I want you to be part of mine."

"Marriage? Is that what you want?" He spun away to lean on the rail. "What the hell is marriage, Maddy?"

"An emotional commitment between two people who promise to do their best."

"For better or for worse." He turned back then, but his face was in shadow and she could only read his voice. "How many of them last?"

"Only the ones that people work hard enough at, I suppose. Only for the ones that care enough."

"Many don't last. The institution doesn't mean anything. It's a legal contract broken by another legal contract, the first of which is usually broken morally dozens of times in between."

Part of her heart broke for him just hearing what he said. "Reed, you can't generalize that way."

"How many happy marriages can you name? How many lasting ones?" he corrected. "Forget the happiness."

"Reed, that's ridiculous. I—"

"Can't even think of one?" he said.

Her temper snapped into place. "Of course I can. The—the Gianellis's on the first floor of my building."

"The ones who shout at each other constantly."

"They like to shout. It makes them deliriously happy to shout." Because she'd begun to shout herself, she spun on her heel and racked her brain. "Damn it, if you weren't quizzing me, I wouldn't have such a hard time at it. Ozzie and Harriet."

"Give it a break, Maddy."

"No." Setting her hands on her hips, she glared at him. "Jimmy Stewart's been married for a hundred and fifty years. Umm . . . Queen Elizabeth and Prince Philip are doing pretty good. My parents, for God's sake," she continued, warming up. "They've been together forever. My great-aunt Jo was married for fifty-five years."

"Had to work at it, didn't you?" He came out of the shadows then, and what she saw in his eyes was cynicism. "You'd have an easier time coming up with marriages that crumbled."

"All right, I would. It doesn't mean you give up on the system because the people involved in it make mistakes. Besides, I didn't ask you to marry me, I just asked you to feel."

He caught her before she could storm inside again. "Are you going to tell me marriage isn't what you want?"

She stood toe-to-toe with him. "No, I'm not going to tell you that."

"I can't promise marriage. I admire you, as a woman and as a performer. I'm attracted to you . . . I need you."

"All those things are important, Reed, but they're only enough for a little while. If I hadn't fallen in love with you, we could both be happy with that. I don't think I can handle too much more." She turned and gripped the railing as if it were a lifeline. "Please, just go."

It wasn't easy to fight her when he seemed to be fighting himself, as well. The moves weren't clear, the next step wasn't as well defined as it should have been. Seeing no other way, Reed backed off. "It's not finished. No matter how much both of us would like it otherwise."

"Maybe not." She drew in a breath. "But I've made a fool of myself in front of you for the last time. Leave me alone now."

The moment he left, she shut her eyes tight. She would *not* cry. As soon as she could pull herself together, she was going back inside to make her excuses and go home. She wasn't running away, she was simply facing reality.

"Maddy."

She turned and faced Edwin. One look told her she didn't need to paste on a bright smile.

"I'm sorry. I listened to a great deal of that, and you've a right to be angry with me. But Reed's my son and I love him."

"I'm not angry." Indeed, she found she couldn't dredge up any emotions at all. "I just have to go."

"I'll take you home."

"No, you have guests." She gestured inside. "I'll catch a cab."

"They'll never miss me." He stepped forward to take her arm. "I want to take you home, Maddy. There's a story you should hear."

They spoke very little on the way home. Edwin seemed to be lost in thoughts of his own. Maddy had lost her knack for bright, witty conversation. His only comment as they started up the stairs to her apartment was on the lack of security.

"You're becoming more well-known every time you step out onstage, Maddy. There's a price to be paid for that."

She glanced around the dimly lighted hallway as she reached for her keys. She'd never been afraid here, yet somehow she'd known that her time in the free-moving, transient world of the gypsies was almost up.

"I'll fix tea." She left Edwin to wander the cramped living room.

"This suits you, Maddy," he said a few moments later. "It's friendly, bright, honest." The glow of neon made him smile as he settled into a chair. "I'm going to embarrass you and tell you how much I admire what you've done with your life.''

"You don't embarrass me. I appreciate it."

"Talent isn't always enough. I know. I've watched many, many talented people slip away into oblivion because they didn't have the strength or the confidence to make it to the top. You're there, and you haven't even noticed yet."

"I don't know about my reaching the top." She skirted the breakfront carrying a tray. "But I'm happy where I am."

"That's the beauty of it, Maddy. You like where you are. You like yourself." He accepted the cup of tea but put a hand lightly on hers. "Reed needs you."

"Maybe on some levels." She retreated a little, because it hurt too much. "I found out that I need more than that."

"So does he, Maddy. So does he, but he's too stubborn, and maybe too afraid, to admit it."

"I don't understand why. I don't understand how he can be so—" She cut herself off, swearing. "I'm sorry."

"Don't be. I think I understand. Maddy, has Reed ever told you about his mother?"

"No. That's one of the hands-off subjects between us."

"I think you have a right to know." He sighed and sipped his tea, knowing he was about to stir unwanted and painful memories of his own. "If I weren't sure you really cared for him, and that you were really right for him, I could never tell you this."

"Edwin, I don't want you to tell me something Reed would resent me knowing."

"Your concern for him is why I'm going to tell you." He set down his cup and leaned forward. Something told Maddy there would be no going back. "Reed's mother was a stunning woman. Is a stunning woman still, I'm sure, though I haven't seen her in many years."

"Has Reed?"

"No, he refuses to."

"Refuses to see his mother? How could he?"

"Once I explain, maybe you'll understand." There was a weariness in his voice that made her heart go out to him without question.

"I married Elaine when we were both very young. I had some family money, and she was a struggling singer, working the clubs... You understand."

"Yes, of course."

"She had talent, nothing show-stopping, but with the right management she could have made a solid living. I decided to give her that right management. Then I decided to marry her. It was almost as calculated as that, I'm sorry to say, because I was used to getting what I wanted. For a year or two, it worked. She was grateful for what I was doing for her career. I was grateful to have a beautiful wife. I loved her, and I worked very hard to make her a success because that's what she wanted most. Somewhere along the line, things began to change. Elaine was impatient."

Edwin sat back again, sipping tea as he looked around Maddy's apartment. He'd given his wife all he could, yet she'd never been satisfied.

"She was young," he said, knowing it was no real excuse. "She wanted better bookings and began to resent the fact that I was advising her on her clothes, her hair. She began to think that I was holding her back, using her to further my own career."

"She couldn't have understood you very well."

He smiled at that. Not everyone was willing to give such unconditional support. "Perhaps not. But then, I didn't understand her, either. Our marriage was in trouble. I'd almost accepted the fact that it was ending when she told me she was going to have a child. You're a modern woman, Maddy. And a compassionate one. You should be able to understand that while I very much wanted children, had always wanted them, Elaine didn't."

Maddy looked down at her tea, sympathizing with Edwin. "I can only feel sorry for someone who didn't, or for whatever reason couldn't, want the child she carried."

It was the right answer. He closed his eyes on it. "Elaine was desperate for success. She had Reed, I think, because she was afraid to do otherwise. I had gotten her a small recording contract. Her decision to stay with me and have Reed was more a career move than anything else."

"You still loved her."

"I still had feelings for her. And there was Reed. When he was born, I felt as though I'd been given the greatest gift. A son. Someone who would love me, accept the love I wanted to give back. He was beautiful, a wonderful baby who grew into a wonderful child. My life changed the moment he was born. I wanted to give him everything. I had a kind of focus that hadn't been there before. I could lose a client, I could lose a contract, but my son was always there."

"Families keep our feet on the ground."

"Yes, they do. Before I go on, I want you to know that Reed has never given me anything but pleasure. I never considered him a duty or a burden."

"You don't have to tell me that. I can see it."

He rubbed his hand over his temple, then continued. "When he was five, I was in an accident. They did a lot of tests on me in the hospital." His voice was changing. Maddy tensed without knowing why. "One of the by-products of the testing was a report that I was sterile."

Her hand grew damp on the cup, and she set it down. "I don't understand."

"I couldn't have children." His eyes were direct, intense. "I'd never been able to have them."

The cold gripped her, squeezing her stomach into a frigid knot. "Reed." With the one word she asked all the questions and gave nothing but love.

"I didn't father him. It was a blow I can't describe to you."

"Oh, Edwin." She rose immediately to kneel in front of him.

"I confronted Elaine. She didn't even try to lie. I think she'd grown tired of the lies by then. The marriage had been over, and she knew she'd never hit it big as an entertainer. There'd been another man, one who'd left her as soon as he'd learned she was pregnant." His breath came out in a slow, painful stream. "It must have been a terrible blow to her. She'd known I wouldn't question but simply accept the child as mine. Moreover, she'd known, inside she'd known, that she'd never have gotten out of those dreary little clubs without me. So she'd stuck."

"She must have been a very unhappy woman."

"Not everyone finds contentment easily. Elaine was too restless to do anything but look for it. If she wasn't satisfied, she'd move on. When I got out of the hospital, she was gone. Reed was staying with a neighbor." He drew a deep breath because, after all the years that had passed, it still hurt. "Maddy, she'd told him."

"Oh, my God." She dropped her head on his knee and wept for all of them. "Poor little boy."

"I didn't do much better by him." Edwin laid a hand on her hair. He hadn't realized how cleansing it would be to speak of it aloud after all those years. "I needed to get away, so I paid the neighbor and left him there. I was gone nearly a month, pulling money together to finance Valentine Records. Until I met your family, I'm not sure I had any intention of going back. It's hard to forgive myself for that."

"You were hurt. You—"

"Reed was devastated," he said. "I hadn't considered the effect it would have on him. I'd thrown myself into the hustling game and tried to block out what I'd left behind. Then I met your parents. For just one night, I saw what family meant."

Rubbing a hand over her wet cheek, she looked up. "And you slept on a cot in their room."

"I slept on a cot and watched the love your parents had for each other and for their children. It was as though someone had drawn a curtain aside to let me see what life really meant, what was really important. I broke down. Your father took me out to a bar and I told him everything. God knows why."

"Pop's easy to talk to."

"He listened to all of it, sympathized some, but not as much as I thought I deserved." After all the years that had passed, Edwin could remember and even laugh a little. "He had a shot of whiskey in his hand. He downed it, slapped me on the shoulder and told me I had a son to think of and that I should go home to him. He saw clean through it, and he was right. I've never forgotten what he did for me just by speaking the truth."

She took his hands now, holding tight. "And Reed?"

"He was my son, always had been, always would be my son. I was a fool to have forgotten that."

"You hadn't forgotten," she murmured. "I don't think you'd forgotten."

"No." He felt the smoothness and strength of her hands in his. "In my heart I hadn't. I drove back. He was playing in the yard alone. This boy, not quite six, turned and looked at me with adult eyes." A shudder moved through him, quick and violent. "I've never been able to wipe out that one moment when I saw what his mother and I had done to him."

"You've no cause to blame yourself. No," she added before Edwin could speak again. "I've seen you and Reed together. You've no cause to blame yourself."

"I did everything I could to make it up to him, to make things normal. In fact, it didn't take me very long to forget what his mother had done. Reed never forgot. He still carries that bitterness, Maddy, that I saw in his eyes when he was five years old."

"What you've told me helps me to understand a great deal." Taking a deep breath, she sat back on her heels. "But, Edwin, I don't know what I can do."

"You love him, don't you?"

"Yes, I love him."

"You've given him something. He's beginning to trust in someone. Don't take it away now."

"He doesn't want what I have to give him."

"He does, and he'll come around. Just don't give up on him."

She rose and wrapped her arms around herself, then turned away. "Are you so sure I'm what he needs?"

"He's my son." As she turned back slowly, Edwin rose. "Yes, I'm sure."

He wasn't asleep. He couldn't sleep. Reed had nearly given in to the urge to lose himself in a bottle of Scotch, but he decided misery was better company.

He'd lost her. Because they hadn't been able to accept each other for what they were, he'd lost her. Oh, she was better off without him. That he was certain of. Yet, she'd been the best thing that had ever happened to him.

He'd hurt her, just as he'd known he would, but wasn't it strange how much he hurt, too?

She'd be gone tomorrow, he told himself. The best thing to do was to forget, and to put the handling of the play and the cast album in his father's hands. He'd divorce himself from it, and therefore purge himself of memories of Maddy O'Hurley.

He started to cross to the windows but remembered how Maddy had been drawn to them. Swearing, he paced away again.

The knock on the door surprised him. He didn't often have visitors at one in the morning. He didn't want visitors, he thought, and ignored the knock. It continued to sound stubbornly. Annoyed, Reed yanked the door open with the intention of blasting anyone who had the misfortune to be there.

"Hi." Maddy stood with a dance bag slung over her shoulders and her hands dipped into the pockets of a wide denim skirt.

"Maddy—"

"I was in the neighborhood," she began, and walked past him into the apartment. "I decided to drop in. I didn't wake you, did I?"

"No, I—"

"Good. I'm always cranky when someone wakes me up. So..." She tossed her bag down. "How about a drink?"

"What are you doing here?"

"I told you I was in the neighborhood."

Crossing to her, he held her by the shoulders and kept her still. "What are you doing here?"

She tilted her head. "I couldn't keep away from you."

Before he could prevent it, his hand had reached for her cheek. He dropped it again. "Maddy, a few hours ago—"

"I said a lot of things," she finished for him. "They were all true. I love you, Reed. I want to marry you. I want to spend my life with you. And I think we could do a pretty good job of it. But until you think so, we'll just have to coast."

"You're making a mistake."

She rolled her eyes. "Reed, you're putting those scratchy clothes on me again. If we were married, maybe—just maybe—you could suggest what was best for me. As things stand, I make my own decisions. I really would like a drink. Got any diet soda?"

"No."

"All right, whiskey then. Reed, it's very rude to refuse to serve a guest a drink."

He continued to hold her a moment longer, then gave in and lowered his forehead to hers. "I do need you, Maddy."

"I know." She lifted her hands to his face. "I know you do. I'm glad you know it."

"If I could give you what you wanted—"

"We've talked about it enough for now. I'm leaving for Philadelphia tomorrow."

"Dancing to the piper," he murmured.

"That's right, and I'm going to work my tail off, so I don't want to talk. I don't want to argue, not tonight."

"All right. I'll get us a drink."

He moved over to the bar and chose a decanter. "You know, Reed, it's still a very odd feeling for me to take my clothes off onstage."

He had to laugh. Somehow she always made him laugh. "I imagine it is."

"I mean, I wear a bodysuit and spangles and don't expose more than I would on a public beach, but it's the act itself that's odd. I have to pull this off in front of several hundred people in a few days. That means practice, practice, practice."

When he turned back, she was smiling at him and slowly unbuttoning her blouse. "I thought you might give me an unbiased opinion on my...stage presence. Stripping's an art, you know." She ran a hand down the center of her body as her blouse parted. "Titillating..." She turned her back and looked at him over her shoulder. "Fanciful." She let the blouse slip gently away. "What do you think?"

"I think you're doing great. So far."

"I just want to be sure I make Mary realistic." She loosened the tie on her skirt and let it fall as she turned back. The brief black merry widow she wore had him setting down his glass before he dropped it.

"I've never seen you wear anything like that."

"This?" She passed a hand down her body again. "Not really my style. Not comfortable enough. But for Mary..." She bent from the waist and unhooked a garter from the sheer black stocking. "It's sort of a trademark." She straightened again and ran both hands through her hair in an upward motion. "Do you think it'll sell?"

"I'm thinking that if you wear that onstage I'll strangle you."

With a laugh, she unhooked the second garter, then slowly rolled the stocking down her leg. "You have to remember I'm Mary once the curtain's up. And I'm going to help make your play a hit." She tossed the stocking at him, then began the same routine on the other. "It's too bad I don't have a more voluptuous figure."

"Yours does very well."

"Do you think?" Still smiling, she began to unhook the lace covering her breasts. "Reed, I hate to be a pest, but you haven't given me that drink."

"Sorry." He picked up her glass and carried it to her.

Maddy took it, and for a moment the humor in her eyes turned into something deeper. "This one's for my Pop," she said, and touched her glass to his.

"What?"

"You don't have to understand." She smiled again and tossed back the shot of whiskey. It poured through her like lava. "What do you think of the show so far? Worth the price of a ticket?"

He'd meant to be gentle. He'd wanted to be tender to show her how much her coming back to him meant. But the hands that dived into her hair were tense and urgent. "I've never wanted you more."

She tilted her head back and let her empty glass fall carelessly to the carpet. "Show me."

He dragged her against him, desperate. The sting of whiskey clung to her lips, intoxicating. Her arms went around him, welcoming the rage of desire. It was the first time, the only time, she had felt him come to her without control. Her blood began to pound with anticipation of facing unleashed passion. When he pulled her to the floor, she went willingly.

His hands were everywhere, touching, stroking, pressing. He lifted her up to a blinding peak where she could only gasp his name and ask for more.

There was more, much more.

Impatient, he tugged at the remaining hooks, freeing her body to his. Just as urgent, her fingers tore at the belt of his robe until she found warm, naked flesh and muscle.

The carpet was smooth at her back. His body was hard against hers. She heard her name whispered through his lips, harshly. Then he was filling her.

It had never been so fast before, so furious, so unrestrained. Heedlessly she threw herself into the whirl of pleasure. Her body shook, and so did his. Love and passion mixed so intimately that she couldn't tell one from the other and no longer tried.

She was there for him. As long as he accepted her arms around him, he was there for her.

Chapter Ten

We'd be better off walking.''

Maddy slowed and steered through yet another pothole before she tossed a grin at Wanda. "Where's your sense of adventure?"

"I lost it a mile back in that ditch we went through."

"It wasn't a ditch," Maddy corrected as she maneuvered her way through downtown Philadelphia traffic. "Why don't you look out the window and tell me when we pass something of great historical significance?"

"I can't look out the window." Wanda folded her long legs into a more comfortable position. It wasn't easy, as Maddy had chosen to rent a nifty little compact with bucket seats that all but sat on the dash. "It makes me seasick when the buildings bounce up and down."

"It's not the buildings, it's the car."

"That, too." Wanda grabbed the doorhandle for support. "Why did you rent this heap, anyway?"

"Because I never get to drive in New York. Is that Independence Hall?" When Maddy craned her neck around, Wanda gave her a none-too-gentle shove on the shoulder.

"Honey, you watch the road if you want to get back to New York."

Maddy bumped to a stop at a light. "I like driving," she said breezily.

"Some people like jumping out of planes," Wanda muttered.

"I'd have a car in New York if I thought I would ever have a chance to use it. How much time do we have?"

"Fifteen fun-filled minutes." Wanda braced herself as Maddy shot forward again. "I know I should have asked this before I got in the car, but when's the last time you drove?"

"Oh, I don't know. A year. Maybe two. I think we should try some of those little shops on South Street after rehearsal."

"If we live to see it," Wanda mumbled, then pressed the invisible brake on her side as Maddy whipped around a sedan. "You know, Maddy, the man on the street probably would think you're about the happiest human being alive. Somebody who knows you a bit better might tell you that your smile's going to crack around the edges if you don't ease up."

Maddy downshifted as the car jittered over yet another pothole. "That obvious?"

"Obvious enough. What's going on with you and Mr. Wonderful?"

Maddy let out a long, sighing breath. "One day at a time."

"And you're the type who needs to have a good grip on next week."

It was true, too true, but she shook her head. "He has a good reason for feeling the way he does."

"But that doesn't change the way you feel."

"I guess not. You know, Wanda, I never really used to believe it when people said life was complicated. Stop me if I get too personal," she began, and Wanda merely shrugged. "When you were married before, did you think it was forever?"

Wanda pursed her lips. "I guess you could say I did and he didn't."

"Well, would you ... I mean, if you met someone you really cared about, would you get married?"

"Again?" Instinctively Wanda started to laugh, then thought better of it. "If there was someone who made everything click, I might do it. But I'd think about it for longer. No, hell, I wouldn't, either. I'd dive in with both feet."

"Why?"

"Because there aren't any guarantees. If I thought I had a chance, I'd take it. Like the lottery. Weren't you suppose to turn there?"

"Turn? Oh, damn." Muttering to herself, Maddy bumped her way around the block. "Now we'll be late."

"Better that you get what's on your mind out of your system first, anyway."

"I was just hoping he'd be here." Maddy turned again and got back on track. "I know he couldn't very well spend the whole week down here while we're in rehearsal, but we'd kind of planned that he would come today."

"No-show?"

"Something came up. He was vague about it, something about some problem with playlists and promoters or something."

"We've all got a job to do, kid."

"Yeah." With maneuvering even Wanda had to admire, Maddy squeezed into a minuscule parking space right across from the theater. "I guess I better think about my own. Two more full rehearsals and we're on."

"Don't remind me." Wanda set a hand on her stomach. "Every time I think about it a 747 lands in my gut."

"You're going to be great." Maddy stepped out of the car and slammed the door. At the end of the block, someone was selling cut flowers. She made a mental note to treat herself after rehearsal. "*We're* going to be great."

"I'm going to hold you to that. The last play I was in closed after two performances. I gave serious thought to sticking my head in the oven. But it was electric."

"Tell you what." Maddy paused by the stage door and grinned. "If we flop, you can use mine. I've got gas."

"Thanks a lot."

"That's what friends are for." Maddy pushed open the door, took one step inside, then let out a whoop. With some curiosity, Wanda watched her launch down the corridor and fling herself at a group of people.

"You're here. You're all here."

"And where else would we be?" Frank O'Hurley picked up his baby girl and swung her in a circle.

"But all of you!" The minute her feet touched the floor, Maddy grabbed her mother and squeezed her ribs until they threatened to crack. "You look great, absolutely great."

"So do you." Molly returned the hug. "And late for rehearsal, as usual."

"Missed my turn driving here. Oh, Abby." She reached for her sister, hugged and held on. "I'm so glad you could come. I was afraid you wouldn't be able to get away from the farm."

"It'll be there when we get back. How often does my sister have an opening night?" But concern clouded Abby's eyes. She knew her sister as well as she knew herself, and she didn't think the tension she felt from Maddy had anything to do with professional nerves.

Still hugging Abby, Maddy grabbed for her brother-in-law's hand. "Dylan, thanks for bringing her."

"I think it was the other way around." With a laugh, he kissed Maddy's cheek. "But you're welcome."

"It's too bad," she began with a wink to Abby, "that you couldn't bring the boys."

"We're right here."

Deliberately Maddy looked in the opposite direction. "Did I hear something?"

"We came, too."

"We're going to New York."

"I could have sworn I..." Maddy let her words trail off as she focused on her nephews. Carefully she kept her face blank for a moment, then widened her eyes. "You can't be Ben and Chris—can you? They're just little boys. You're both much too tall to be Ben and Chris.''

"We are too," Chris piped up. "We grew."

Taking her time, Maddy studied both of them. "No fooling?"

"Come on, Maddy." Though he tried not to look too pleased, Ben grinned and shuffled his feet. "You know it's us."

"You're going to have to prove it to me. Give me a hug."

She bent down to hold them both tight. "We rode on a plane," Chris began. "I got to sit by the window."

"Miss O'Hurley, they want you in Wardrobe."

"Shoot." Maddy released her nephews and straightened. "Look, where are you all staying? There's a whole list of hotels on the call board. I can—"

"We're booked in your hotel," Molly told her. "Now go on, we'll have plenty of time."

"Okay. Are you going to stay for rehearsal?"

"Think they could stop us?" Frank asked.

When she heard her name again, she started down the hall, walking backward to keep them in view just a moment longer. "As soon as I'm done, we're going to celebrate. I'm buying."

Frank chuckled and draped an arm over his wife's shoulders. "Does she think we'd argue with that? Let's go get a front-row seat."

"Mr. Selby to see you, sir." Hannah kept a cool, professional smile on her face as she ushered Selby into Reed's office.

"Thank you, Hannah. Hold my calls." There would be no tray of coffee and sweet rolls today. Reed caught Hannah's look of disapproval before she shut the door. "Sit down, Selby."

"I guess your old man's proud of you." Selby cast a look around the office before he settled himself comfortably. "You've kept the label right up top. Heard you signed that little group from D.C. A risky move."

Reed merely lifted a brow and held his gaze steady. He knew Galloway had offered the group a contract. Valentine had simply offered them a better one. "We don't mind a few risks."

"Always a headache to get the stations to put new talent on their playlist. A record from an unknown's going to die without solid promotion." Selby took out a small, thin cigar, then fiddled with his lighter. "That's why I'm here. I thought it would be wise if we talked before the RIAA meeting this afternoon."

Reed continued to sit back, waiting for Selby to light his cigar. He'd known as soon as Selby had requested an appointment that the other man was running scared. The Recording Industry Association of America didn't have closed meetings every day. Those involved were aware that the label heads would vote on whether the organization should investigate independent promoters. Some major record companies, Galloway included, still used the independents, though the shadow of scandal, payola and kickbacks lurked around the edges of their profession.

"Look, Valentine," Selby began when Reed remained silent. "Neither of us started in this business yesterday. We know what the bottom line is. Airplay.

Without airplay on the important stations, a record dies.''

He was sweating, Reed observed calmly. Beneath the trendy pastel suit and the sunlamp tan, nerves ran hot. Just what would a full investigation mean to Galloway? Reed speculated.

"When you pay for airplay, Selby, you're riding a sick horse. Sooner or later it's going to fall down under you."

Letting out a quick stream of smoke, Selby leaned forward. "We both know how the system works. If it means slipping a few hundred to a program director, who does it hurt?"

"And if it means threatening that same program director if he doesn't play ball?"

"That's nonsense." But there was a tiny bead of sweat on his temple.

"If it is, an investigation will clear it up. In the meantime, Valentine Records will get its new releases played without independents."

"Throwing the baby out with the bathwater," Selby snapped, then rose. "Top 40 stations report their playlist to the trades. If a new release doesn't hit the trades, it might as well not exist. That's the system."

"Maybe the system needs a little reworking."

"Just as narrow-minded and straight as your old man."

A ghost of a smile touched Reed's lips. "Thank you."

"It's easy for you, isn't it?" Bitter, Selby turned on Reed. "You sit here in your cozy little office, never getting your hands dirty. Your daddy did that for you."

Reed checked his temper. "If you look," he said quietly, "you'll see my father's hands are clean. Valentine doesn't, and never has, run its business on payola, kickbacks or heavy-handed threats."

"You're not so lily-white, Valentine."

"Let's just say that in an hour Valentine Records will vote for a full investigation."

"It'll never fly." Selby smirked as he crushed out his cigar, but his hands weren't steady. He'd come to Reed because Valentine had the reputation and power to sway the vote. Now he was choking. Selby loosened the careful knot of his tie. "Too many labels know where the bread's buttered. Even if you probe, I won't lose. Oh, a few heads will roll down the line, but mine won't. Ten years ago, Galloway was a hole-in-the-wall. Today it's one of the top names in the business. I made it because I played the game, I watched the angles. When the dust settles, Valentine, I'm still going to be on top."

"I'm sure you will," Reed murmured as Selby stormed out of his office. Men like that never paid for their actions. They had plenty of fall guys and scapegoats littering their path. If Reed had wanted a personal vendetta, he could have initiated an investigation of his own. Already he had information on a disc jockey who'd been beaten, allegedly for not playing certain releases. There was the program director in New Jersey whose wife had been threatened. There was another who made frequent trips to Vegas, traveling first-class and gambling heavily. More heavily than his annual salary would permit. Part of the game. Not a game Reed cared to play.

But it was unlikely Selby would pay for his actions. Did anyone?

Rising, he checked the contents of his briefcase. It was true that he had come into a business that had already been well established. He hadn't had to hustle his way to a label. If he had, would he have scrambled for a shortcut? Because he didn't know, couldn't be sure, Reed decided to leave the investigation up to the RIAA. He'd let the dust settle. It would be a long, probably ugly meeting, Reed thought as he stepped out of his office.

"I won't be back today, Hannah."

"Good luck, Mr. Valentine. You had a few calls while you were talking to that man."

His mouth twitched a little at her tone. "Anything important?"

"No, nothing that can't wait. You did get a call from Miss O'Hurley." Hannah sent him an entirely-too-innocent smile and hoped for a reaction. The fact that he hesitated told Hannah everything she needed to know.

"If she calls back, tell her . . ."

"Yes, Mr. Valentine?"

"Tell her I'll get back to her."

Disappointment ruled for a moment. "Ah, Mr. Valentine?"

"Yes?"

She could see the impatience, but pressed just a little further. "I wondered if you were going to Philadelphia for the opening, or if perhaps you'd like me to send flowers."

He thought of the meeting he had to deal with, of the work that couldn't be ignored. He thought of Maddy's face and the confusion that had been dogging him for days. Her feelings, his, his needs, hers.

Were they really the same, or were they so totally opposed that they could never come together?

"My father's going. If I don't, we'll be represented."

"I see," Hannah said primly, and stacked papers on her desk.

"I'll take care of the flowers myself."

"See that you do," she muttered as he went out the glass doors.

It had gone well. Maddy dropped crosswise on her bed and let the rehearsal play back in her head. She wouldn't jinx it by saying it was perfect, but she could think it. As long as she thought it very quietly.

Tomorrow night. Tomorrow night at this time, she thought with a little skip of the pulse, she'd be in her dressing room. Twenty-four hours. She rolled onto her back and stared at the ceiling. How in the hell was she going to get through the next twenty-four hours?

He hadn't called back. Maddy shifted her head so that she could look at the phone again. They had only spoken to each other a handful of times since she'd left for Philadelphia, and every time they had she'd sensed he was trying to distance himself from her. Maybe he'd succeeded.

A dancer was no stranger to pain. You felt it, acknowledged it, then went on and worked around it. Heartache might be a little more difficult to deal with than a pulled muscle, but she would go on. Survive. She'd always prided herself on being a survivor.

Her family was here. Rousing herself from the bed, Maddy went to the closet. She would change, put on her happiest face and take her family out on the town. Not everyone was as lucky as she, Maddy reminded herself as she stripped out of her sweats. She had a family who loved her, who stood behind her, who thought she was just fine the way she was.

She had a career that was on the rise. Even if she lost her grip on the brass ring, no one could take her dancing away from her. If she had to go back and play the clubs again, do regional theater, summer stock, she'd still be happy.

Maddy O'Hurley didn't need a man to complete her life, because her life was complete. She didn't want a knight on a white charger to scoop her up and take her away from all this. She liked where she was, who she was.

If Reed backed out of her life, she could— She leaned back against the closet door with a sigh. She could very possibly be the most miserable person alive. No, she didn't need him to save or protect her. She needed him to love her, and though she didn't think he could understand, she needed him to let her love him.

When she heard the knock on her door, Maddy shook herself out of what was dangerously close to depression. "Who is it?"

"It's Abby."

Leaving her robe untied, Maddy dashed to the door. Abby stood there, looking fresh and quietly lovely in a slim white dress. "Oh, you're all ready. I haven't even started."

"I dressed early so I could come down and talk."

"Before you say anything, I have to tell you how wonderful you look. Maybe it's Dylan, maybe it's the country air, but you've never looked better."

"Maybe it's pregnancy."

"What?"

"I found out right before we left home." She took Maddy by the shoulders, looking as though she could take on the world. "I'm going to have another baby."

"Oh, God. Oh, Abby, that's great. I'm going to cry."

"Okay. Let's sit down while you do."

Maddy searched fruitlessly in her robe pocket for tissue. "How does Dylan feel about it?"

"Stunned." Abby laughed as they sat together on the bed. Her eyes were soft. The hint of rose under her skin enhanced the curve of her cheeks. She pushed her wavy blond hair behind her back before she took Maddy's hands. "We're going to make the announcement at dinner tonight."

"And you're going to start taking better care of yourself. No more mucking out the stalls. I mean it, Abby," she continued before her sister could speak. "If I have to lecture Dylan, I will."

"You don't have to. He'd like to wrap me up in tissue for the next seven months or so. We weren't made for that, Maddy, you know we weren't."

"Maybe not, but you can ease off." She threw her arms around her sister and squeezed. "I'm so happy for you."

"I know. Now I want you to talk to me." Firm, Abby straightened her back. "Chantel called me and said you were making yourself crazy over some man."

"She would," Maddy muttered. "I'm not making myself crazy over anything. It's not my style."

Abby slipped off her shoes. "Who is he?"

"His name's Reed Valentine."

"Valentine Records?"

"That's right. How do you know?"

"I still keep up with the industry a little. And Dylan worked with him on a book some time ago."

"Yes, Reed mentioned it."

"And?"

"And nothing. I met him, I fell in love with him, I made a fool of myself." She tried to keep her voice careless and light, and nearly succeeded. "Now I'm sitting here staring at the phone waiting for him to call. Like a teenager."

"You never had much of a chance to be a teenager when you were sixteen."

"I don't care much for it. He's a good man, Abby. Kind and gentle, though he'd never see that in himself. Can I tell you about him?"

"You know you can."

She started at the beginning and left nothing out. It never occurred to her that she was betraying Reed's privacy. In truth, she wasn't. Whatever she said to Abby or to Chantel was like telling her thoughts to herself.

Abby listened in her calm, serene way while Maddy told her everything; the love, the compromises, the trauma that had marred Reed's childhood and affected his life. Because they were so in tune with each other, Abby hurt when her sister did.

"So you see, no matter how much I love him, I can't change what happened to him or how he feels."

"I'm sorry." They shifted together, with Abby's arm around Maddy's shoulder. "I know how painful it is. I can only tell you that I know absolutely that if you love hard enough you can work miracles. Dylan didn't want to love me. The truth is, I didn't want to love him, either." It was easy to look back and remember. "We'd both made a decision never to risk that kind of involvement again. It was a very logical decision made by two intelligent people." She smiled a little, leaning her head against Maddy's. "Love has a way of wiping out everything but what really matters."

"I've tried to tell myself that. But Abby, he wasn't dishonest with me. Right from the start he made it clear that he didn't want to get involved. It was to be a very casual relationship, which of course isn't a relationship at all. I'm the one who stepped over the line, so I'm the one who had to make the adjustments."

"That's also very logical. What happened to your optimism, Maddy?"

"I left it in a drawer at home."

"Then it's time you pulled it out again. This isn't like you, mooning around, looking at the dark side. You were the one who always planted her feet and refused to budge until things worked out your way."

"This is different."

"No, it's not. Don't you know how much I've always wanted to be as confident of myself as you are? I always envied that quality in you Maddy, when day after day I went on, afraid of failing."

"Oh, Abby."

"It's true, and you can't let me down now. If you love him, really love him, then you've got to plant your feet until he can admit he loves you, too."

"He has to feel it first, Abby."

"I think he does." She gave her sister a quick shake. "Go back over everything you've just told me, but this time listen. The man's crazy about you, Maddy, he just hasn't been able to admit it to you or to himself."

Hope, never far beneath the surface, began to stir again. "I've tried to believe that."

"Don't try, do. I've had the worst a relationship can offer, Maddy. Now I'm having a taste of the best." Instinctively she rested a hand on her stomach, where a new life slept. "Don't give up. But I'll be damned if I'm going to sit here and watch you wait for him to toss you a few crumbs. Get dressed," Abby ordered. "We're going to celebrate."

"Bossy." Maddy grinned as she walked to her closet. "You always were bossy."

Reed let the phone ring a dozen times before he hung up. It was nearly midnight. Where the hell was she? Why wasn't she in bed, resting up for the next day? The one thing he knew about her, was absolutely certain of, was that Maddy trained for a part as rigorously as an athlete. Training meant diet, exercise, attitude and rest. So where the hell was she?

In Philadelphia, he thought, disgusted as he walked to the windows and back again. She was miles away in Philadelphia, in her own world, with her own people. She could be doing anything, with anyone. And he had no right to question her.

The hell with rights, he told himself as he picked up the phone again. She was the one who spoke of love, of commitments, of trust. And she was the one not answering her phone.

He could still remember how disappointed she'd looked when he'd told her he couldn't be sure he'd be there for opening night. He'd had the damn RIAA meeting hanging over his head, and he still couldn't judge the backlash from it. There was bound to be a scandal now that the investigation had been approved. A scandal would affect everyone, every label, every record company executive, even the ones who'd kept their noses clean.

In the morning he was likely to have dozens of calls, from reporters, radio stations, consulting firms, his own employees. He couldn't very well drop everything and go off to watch the opening of a play.

Not just any play, he thought as the phone rang on and on. Maddy's play. No, his play, Reed reminded himself as he slammed the phone down again. Valentine Records was backing it and therefore had a duty to protect its interests. His father would be there, that would be enough. But *he* was president of Valentine, Reed reminded himself.

Was he excusing himself from going or from remaining behind?

It really didn't matter. None if it really mattered at all. What mattered was why Maddy wasn't answering the phone at midnight.

She had a right to her own life.

The hell she did.

Reed ran a hand through his hair. He was acting like a fool. Trying to calm himself, he walked over to pour himself a drink, and the plant caught his eye. There were new green shoots spreading out, young and healthy. The old, yellowed leaves had fallen off and been swept away. Compelled, he reached out to stroke one of the smooth, heart-shaped leaves.

A minor miracle? Perhaps, but it was only a plant, after all. A very stubborn plant, he conceded. One that had refused to die when it should have, one that had responded wholeheartedly to the proper care and attention.

So he had luck with plants. Deliberately, he turned away and stared at his empty apartment. It wouldn't be wise to make too much of its having been Maddy's. Just as it wasn't wise to make too much out of the fact that she wasn't in her room. He had other things to think about, other things to do. But he left the drink untouched.

The room was pitch-dark when knocking disturbed her sleep. Maddy rolled over, snuggled into the pillow and prepared to ignore it. When it continued, she shook herself awake, half believing it was a cue.

It was the middle of the night, she reminded herself with a huge yawn. She had hours yet before she had to step out onstage. But the knocking was definitely at her door and getting louder every minute.

"All right!" she called out irritably, and rubbed her eyes open. If one of the dancers had the jitters, she was going to send her back to her own room to sleep it off. She couldn't afford to be a pillar of strength at three a.m.

"Just hang on, will you?" Muttering, she found the light switch, then hunted up a robe. She unlocked her door, then pulled it open until the chain snapped into place. "Now look...Reed!" Instantly awake, Maddy slammed the door in his face and fumbled with the chain. When she pulled it open again, she jumped into his arms. "You're here! I didn't think you'd be here. I'd nearly gotten used to the idea that you weren't coming. No, I hadn't," she corrected immediately, and found his lips with hers. She felt it—the need, the tension. "Reed, what are you doing here at three in the morning?"

"Do you mind if I come in?"

"Of course not." She stepped back and waited while he tossed a small overnight bag on a chair. "Is something wrong?" she began, then tugged at his shirt. "Oh, God, is something wrong with your father? Reed—"

"No, my father's fine. He should be here tomorrow."

Her fingers relaxed but stayed where they were. "You're upset."

"I'm fine." He moved back from her and walked around the room. She'd already made it her own, he noticed, with tights, socks, shoes strewn here and there. The dresser was a rubble of bottles and pots and scraps of paper. She'd spilled a bit of powder and hadn't bothered to dust it off. He ran a finger through it, and her scent clung to his skin. "I couldn't reach you tonight."

"Oh? I was out having dinner with—"

"You don't owe me an explanation." Furious, though only with himself, he whirled around.

She pushed the hair away from her face and wished she understood him. It was three in the morning, she reminded herself. He was obviously edgy. She was tired. It would be best to take it slow.

"All right. Reed, you're not going to tell me you drove all the way to Philadelphia because I didn't answer the phone." Even as he stared at her, he saw puzzlement turn to humor and humor to pleasure. "You did?" Going to him, she slipped her arms around him, pressing her cheek to his chest. "That's about the nicest thing anyone's ever done for me. I don't know what to say. I—" But when she looked up, she saw it in his eyes. All the pleasure drained from hers as she backed away.

"You thought I was with someone else." Her voice was very quiet, the words very distinct. "You thought I was sleeping with someone else, so you came to see for yourself." A bitter taste rose in her throat. It was a taste she'd rarely sampled. She gestured toward the empty bed. "Sorry to disappoint you."

"Don't." He grabbed her wrist before she could turn away, because he'd already seen the tears welling in her eyes. "That wasn't it. Or—damn it, maybe it was part of it, part of what went through my mind. You'd have a perfect right."

"Thank you." She pulled her wrist away and sat on the edge of the bed, but she couldn't stop the tears. "Now that you've satisfied yourself, why don't you go? I need my sleep."

"I know." He ran both hands though his hair before he sat beside her. "I know that, and when it was late and I couldn't reach you, I wondered." When her eyes lifted to his, he cursed himself. "All right, I did wonder if you were with someone else. I don't have any hold on you, Maddy."

"You're an idiot."

"I know that, too. Just give me a minute." Anticipating her, Reed took both her hands before she could refuse. "Please. I did wonder, and I hated the idea. Then I worried. The whole time I was driving here I worried that something had happened to you."

"Don't be ridiculous. What could happen?"

"Nothing. Anything." His hands tightened on hers in frustration. "I just had to be here. To see you."

The anger was draining, but she didn't know what would rise up to replace it. "Well, you've seen me. Now what?"

"That's up to you."

"No." She pulled away again and rose. "I want you to tell me. I want you to look at me right now and tell me what it is you want."

"I want you." He rose slowly. "I want you to let me stay. Not to make love with you, Maddy. Just to be here."

She could easily allow the hurt to overwhelm her. She could just as easily toss her hurt feelings aside and reach out to him. With a smile, she stepped closer. "You *don't* want to make love with me?"

"I want to make love with you until we both collapse." Shaken because it was true, he reached out to touch her cheek. "But you need your sleep."

"Worried about your investment?" She ran her fingers down his shirt, unfastening buttons as she went.

"Yes." He took her face in his hands. "Yes, I am."

"You don't have to be." Watching him, she slid his shirt off his shoulders. "Trust me. At least for tonight, trust me."

Chapter Eleven

He wanted to. Somewhere during the long, frustrating night, he'd realized that if he trusted her, what she was, what she said, what she felt, his life would turn around. He just couldn't be certain the answers would be waiting for him if it did.

But her touch was so easy, and her eyes were so warm. For tonight, for just one more night, nothing else really mattered.

He brought her hands, both of them, to his lips, as if he could show her what he didn't feel safe in saying, or feel safe in even thinking. She smiled at him, as always touched by the tenderness he was capable of.

Bright and steady, the light by the bed continued to burn as they lowered themselves onto already rumpled sheets.

Her eyes stayed open, darkening slowly, as he brushed kisses over her face. He stroked his fingers gently across her shoulder where her robe hung loose, up the long line of her throat and to her lips, where they traced the shape. With the tip of her tongue she moistened his skin, inviting, tempting, promising. Then she nipped, catching his fingertip between her teeth and holding it snug while her eyes dared him.

Watching her, he slid his hand up her leg, loitering on the tight, muscular calf, then lingering on the smooth, cool skin of her thigh. He felt her breath catch, then continued moving up, making her shudder once, twice, before he parted her robe and freed her body to his.

"I thought about touching you like this," Reed murmured as he caressed one small, firm breast, "since the last time I touched you this way."

"I wanted you to be here." She let her hands make their own explorations. Slowly, wanting to see the fire leap into his eyes, she drew his slacks over his hips. "Every night when I closed my eyes, I pretended that you'd be here in the morning. Now you will be."

She pressed a kiss to his shoulder, but her hands were never still. Nor were his.

They moved slowly, though not quite lazily, because the passion was too close to the surface. They savored, in silent agreement that they had all the time they needed. No rush, no hurry, no frantic, desperate merging that left the body and mind dazed. Tonight was a night for the soul first.

Desire me...but quietly. Long for me...but gently. Ache for me...but patiently.

The sheets were tangled beneath her, disturbed by the restless night she had barely begun, warmed now by the passionate night she hoped wouldn't end. Their fingers linked, palm against palm, strength against strength, as their lips met for one more long, luxurious kiss.

Of all the food she had recklessly sampled that evening, there had been nothing to compare with the flavor of his kisses. The wine had lacked sparkle, the spices had been bland when compared with the taste of his lips on hers. He could indeed feed her soul. Somehow, in some way, she wanted to feed his. Her arms came around him as she sought to give back a portion of what she was given.

There seemed to be no limit to her generosity. He could feel it flow over him every time he held her. Now, even with the languorous, passionate movements of her body, he felt it pour out of her, quenching his soul's thirst like something cool in the midday heat.

Her body responded with every move, with every request he made. She was there with him, as desirable and urgent a partner as a man could want. But she was also, he knew, there *for* him, something soft and giving a man could sink into and be soothed by. He didn't know how to repay, to give back what she so selflessly offered. He knew only to love her with infinite care.

If it had been possible, she would have told him that was enough, at least for now. There could be no more words when her mind and body were floating so freely. When he touched her skin, she felt ablaze. He murmured her name and her heart rejoiced. When they came together with all the fire and intensity of lovers reunited, love for him consumed her.

By midmorning, Maddy was up and restless, filled with nervous energy. In a matter of hours, it would be make-or-break time, win-or-lose, all-or-nothing. It simply wasn't possible to stay away from the theater.

"I thought you didn't have to be there until late this afternoon," Reed commented as Maddy directed him down the shortcut she'd discovered from hotel to theater.

"There's no rehearsal, but everything's happening today."

"I was under the impression that everything happens tonight."

"Nothing happens tonight without today. The lights, the sets, the drops. Turn right, then right again."

Through a thick stream of traffic, he eased over and followed her directions. "I didn't think performers worried much about the technical points of a show."

"A musical would lose a lot of its punch if it wasn't trimmed properly. Try to picture *The King and I* without the throne room or *La Cage* without the nightclub. There's a space." Leaning out the window, she pointed it out to him. "Will this thing squeeze into that?"

Reed gave her a mild look, then, with a few turns of the wheel, maneuvered his BMW between two other cars parked at the curb. "Will that do?"

"That's great." She leaned over to kiss him. "You're great. I'm glad you're here, Reed. Have I mentioned that?"

"A few times." He cupped a hand around the back of her neck to keep her close. Keeping her close was becoming a priority. "I should have worked harder to talk you into staying in bed. To rest," he added when she lifted her brow. "You're ready to jump out of your skin."

"This is normal opening-night behavior. If I were relaxed, you could worry. Besides, I think you should see what you're paying for. You're not the kind of man who's only interested in the end product. Come on." She was out of the car and waiting on the sidewalk. "You should get a look at backstage."

They went through the stage door together. Maddy waved to the guard, then followed the noise. The electric sound of a saw came briefly, then was gone. For the most part there were voices, some loud, some lowered, some complaining. Men and women, dressed for work, milled around. Some gave orders, others followed them, in what looked to Reed like quiet confusion.

If he had to take bets that they would be ready for curtain in a matter of hours, he'd have called it a long shot. There was no greasepaint here, no glitter. There was dust, a little grime and a lot of sweat.

A man in a headphone stood downstage with his arms spread over his head. He spoke into the mike as he brought his hands a little closer together. A square of light on the backdrop adjusted with the movement.

"You met the lighting director, didn't you?"

"Briefly," Reed said, and watched him move a few feet to stage right.

"All the lights have to be focused, one at a time. He's doing the downstage lights, his assistant will take care of upstage."

"How many lights are there?"

"Dozens."

"The show starts at eight. Shouldn't this have been done already?"

"We made some changes in rehearsal yesterday. Don't worry." She linked an arm through his. "Whether it's done or not, the show will go on at eight."

Reed cast another look around. There were big wooden crates on wheels, some opened, some closed. Coils of cable littered the floor, ladders were set up here and there. On a Genie lift, a man fiddled with lights while another stood back, motioning down with his hands. A dark backdrop lowered slowly, then stopped on his signal.

"They've got to set the highs and lows on the drops," she told him. "They're all weighted, and the crew has to know how far to take them down, how far to bring them up. Come on, I'll show you the fly floor. That's where they make a lot of magic happen."

Maddy weaved her way backstage, around crates and boxes, carefully skirting ladders rather than walking under them. There was more rope dangling, more cable coiled. Reed saw a rubber chicken hanging by a noose next to where two men taped what looked like an electrical box to a wood panel.

"Miss O'Hurley." One of them turned to grin at her. "Looking good."

"Just make sure you make me look good tonight."

There were tall chests lined up along the back wall, most of them plastered with stickers from other shows. Maddy squeezed between the last drop and the chests.

"We have to cross underneath the stage in this theater," she explained. "Not enough room back here. It's better than having to run outside and around to make your next cue."

"Would it be more organized if—"

"This is theater." Maddy took his hand and led him through a narrow doorway. "This is as organized as it gets. Up here." She climbed up a skinny, steep stairway and through another opening.

It looked to Reed like the deck of a ship—one that had weathered a heavy storm. Ropes were everywhere, some as thick as Maddy's wrist, some thin and wiry. They hung from above and spilled out on the floor, without, it seemed to him, any rhyme or reason. A great many were grouped together, slanting up, then down over a long metal pole.

There was a small table wedged into a corner with papers tacked up around it and spread over it, with an overflowing ashtray on top of everything. A few men were tying ropes with the careless skill of veteran sailors. The place smelled of rope, cigarettes and sweat; the familiar scents that lingered in a theater.

"This is a hemp house," she began. "There aren't too many of them left in the States. It's too bad, really. You have more flexibility with rope and sandbags than you do with counterweights. All the moving pieces are handled from up here. The beaded curtain." She put a hand over a group of ropes that was bound together and labeled with a tag. "It weighs over five hundred pounds. When it's time to let it down in the third act, the stage manager cues the flyman verbally through the intercom. The lighting director backs it up with a light cue."

"Sounds simple enough."

"Sure. Unless you've got two or three cues on top of each other or a drop that's so heavy it takes three men on the ropes. This is a big show. The guys up here won't be taking many coffee breaks."

"I don't understand why you know so much."

"I've been in theater all my life." A man came through the doorway, muscled his way around them and began talking to two men who were tying off rope. "Come out on the paint bridge. It's quite a view."

She made her way around the various ropes, hunched under a steel bar and stepped out on a narrow iron platform. Below, stagehands were spread out. Though it looked no more organized from this angle, Reed began to sense a spirit of teamwork.

"If anything up here has to be painted, this is where they do it." She glanced down and shook her head. "Not my kind of job."

A stream of four-letter words rose up from below. A drop descended silently. Then a spotlight began to play on it, widening, then narrowing, then holding steady. Maddy ran her hands back and forth over the rail.

"That's my spot in act one, scene three."

"If I didn't know better, I'd say you were nervous."

"No, I'm not nervous. I'm terrified."

"Why?" He put a hand over hers. "You know what you can do."

"I know what I have done," she corrected. "I haven't done this yet. Tonight, when the curtain goes up, it's the first time. There's your father." Looking down, Maddy let out a long breath. "It looks like he's talking to the general manager of the theater. You should be down there with them."

"No, I should be here with you." He was just beginning to realize how true that was. He hadn't driven to Philadelphia in the middle of the night because he mistrusted her. He hadn't come with her that morning because he didn't have anything better to do. He'd done both because wherever she was, he belonged. She danced to the piper. And, perhaps, so did he. It scared the hell out of him.

Thirty feet above the stage, on a narrow iron platform, he experienced the fear of falling—but not fear of falling physically onto the floor below. "Let's go down." He wanted people around, strangers, noise, anything to distract him from what was blooming inside.

"All right. Oh. It's my family. Look." Nerves were gone, and the pleasure was so deep that she slipped an arm around Reed's waist without being aware that he stiffened. "There's Pop. See the skinny little man who's kibitzing with one of the carpenters? He could run any part of this show—lights, drops, props. He could direct it or choreograph it, but that's never been for him." She beamed down, all admiration and love. "Spotlight, that's for Pop."

"And for you?"

"I'm told I take after him the most. My mother's there. See the pretty woman with the little boy? That's my youngest nephew, Chris. He decided yesterday he wanted to be a lighting man because they get to ride up in the lift. And my sister Abby. Isn't she lovely?"

Reed looked down, focusing on a slender woman with wavy blond hair. There was an air of contentment around her, though she stood in the midst of chaos. She put her hand on the shoulder of another boy and pointed to the house.

"She's showing Ben where they'll be sitting tonight, I imagine. He's really more excited about going to New York tomorrow. Dylan has meetings with his publisher."

Reed watched Dylan reach down, then heft Chris on his shoulders. The little boy's squeals of delight bounced up to them.

"They're great kids." Because she heard the wistfulness in her own voice, she shook it away. She had enough, Maddy reminded herself. "Let's go say hello."

Back down onstage, she skirted around a row of colored lights bolted to the floor. Later that night they would shine for her. Hearing the signal, she took Reed's hand and drew him aside as the beaded curtain made its glittery descent.

"Pretty terrific, isn't it?"

Reed studied the thousands of beads. "It certainly makes a statement."

"We use this during my dream sequence, when I imagine I'm a ballet dancer instead of a stripper, and of course I *pirouette* right into Jonathan's arms. The nice thing about theater—and about dreams—is you can make anything you want happen."

As they walked around another drop, she heard her father's voice ring out.

"Valentine, I'll be damned." Frank O'Hurley, wiry and small, grabbed the huge, husky man in a rough embrace. "My girl told me you'd sprouted wings to back this play." Delighted, Frank drew back and grinned at him. "How many years has it been?"

"Too many." Edwin pumped Frank's hand enthusiastically. "Too damn many. You don't look any older."

"That's because your eyes are."

"And Molly." Edwin bent down to kiss her cheek. "Pretty as ever."

"There's not a thing wrong with your eyes, Edwin," she assured him, and kissed him again. "It's always good to see an old friend."

"I never forgot you. And I never stopped envying you your wife, Frank."

"In that case, I can't let you kiss her again. You might have a harder time remembering my Abby."

"One of the triplets." He took Abby's hand between his meaty ones. "Incredible. Which one—"

"The middle one," she answered easily.

"Maybe it was your diaper I changed."

With a laugh, Abby turned to Dylan. "My husband, Dylan Crosby. Mr. Valentine is obviously an old, intimate friend of the family."

"Crosby. I've read some of your work. Didn't you work with my son on one of your books?"

"Yes, I did." Dylan felt Ben's hand slip into his and linked fingers with him. "You were out of town at the time, so we never met."

"And grandchildren." Edwin sent another look at Frank and Molly before he hunkered down to the boys' level. "A fine pair. How do you do?" He offered his hand formally to each boy. "Here's something else I covet, Frank."

"I've got a soft spot for the little devils," Frank admitted, winking at them. "Abby's going to give us another one next winter."

"Congratulations." It was envy; he couldn't prevent it. But he felt pleasure, as well. "If you don't have plans, I'd like for you all to join me for dinner before the show."

"We're the O'Hurleys," Frank reminded him. "We never have plans that can't be changed. How's your boy, Edwin?"

"He's fine. As a matter of fact, he . . . Well, here he is now. With your daughter."

When Frank turned, a light went on in his head. He saw Maddy with her hand caught in that of a tall, lean man with sculpted features. And he saw the look in her eyes, warm, glowing and a little uncertain. His baby was in love. The quick twist in his heart was part pleasure, part pain. Both feelings softened when Molly's fingers linked with his.

Introductions were made again, and Frank kept his eyes sharply on Reed. If this was the man his baby had chosen, it was up to him to make sure she'd chosen well.

"So you're in charge of Valentine Records," Frank began. He didn't believe in subtle probing. "Doing a good job of it, are you?"

"I like to think so." The man before Reed was like a bantam rooster—small but scrappy. Frank's hairline was receding and his eyes were a stunning blue, and Reed wondered why, when he looked at Frank O'Hurley, he saw Maddy. There was little or no resemblance on the surface. If it was there—and somehow it was—it came from inside. Perhaps that was why he felt himself so drawn to the man and why he worked so hard to keep his distance.

"A lot of responsibility, a record company," Frank went on. "Takes a clever hand at a wheel. A dependable one. Not married, are you, boy?"

Despite himself, Reed felt a smile tugging. "No, I'm not."

"Never have been?"

"Pop, did I show you how we changed the timing for the finale?" Taking his hand, Maddy dragged him into the wings at stage left. "What do you think you're doing?"

"About what?" He grinned and kissed both her cheeks. "God, what a face you've got. Still look like my little turnip."

"Flattery will get you a punch in the nose." She drew him back behind the stage manager's desk as a group of stagehands wheeled out a crate. "You stop pumping Reed that way, Pop. It's so . . . so obvious."

"What's obvious is that you're my baby girl and I have a right to look after you—when I'm around to do it."

With her arms folded, she tilted her head. "Pop, did you do a good job of raising me?"

"I did the best job."

"Would you say I'm a sensible, responsible woman?"

"Damn right you are." Frank puffed out his chest. "I'd punch the first man who said different."

"Good." She kissed him hard. "Then butt out, O'Hurley." She gave his cheek two sharp pats, then walked out onstage again. "I know everyone has things to do this afternoon." She answered her mother's wink. "I'm going up to the rehearsal room to iron out a few kinks."

She warmed up slowly, carefully, stretching her muscles one by one to insure against injury. There was only her. Only her and the wall of mirrors. She could hear the washing machine humming in the wardrobe room across the hall. In the little kitchen down the hall, someone opened and slammed the refrigerator door. Two people from Maintenance were taking a break just outside the door. Their conversation ebbed and flowed as Maddy bent to touch her chin to her knee. There was only her and the wall of mirrors.

It had been Macke's idea to put in the dream sequence, with its balletic overtones. When she'd mentioned that she hadn't been *en pointe* in six months, he'd simply suggested that she dig out her toe shoes and practice. She had. The extra *pointe* classes every week had added hours to her schedule. She could only hope they paid off.

She'd worked, she'd rehearsed, and the moves and music were lodged in her head. Still, if there was one number that gave her the jitters, it was this one.

She'd be alone onstage for the first four minutes. Alone, the lights a filmy blue, the curtain behind her glittering and shimmering. The music would come up... Maddy pushed the button on her tape recorder and set herself in front of the mirrors. Her arms would cross her body, her hands would rest lightly on her own shoulders. Slowly, very slowly, she would rise *en pointe*. And begin.

The bustle outside the door was blanked out. A series of dreamy *pirouettes*. She wasn't Mary now, but Mary's most private dream. *Jeté*, arms extended. It had to look effortless, as if she floated. The bunching muscles, the strain, weren't allowed to show here. She was an illusion, a music-box dancer in tutu and tiara. Fluidity. She imagined her limbs were water, even as the strength rippled through them for a series of *fouet* turns. Her arms came over her head as she went to an *arabesque*. She would hold this for only a few seconds, until Jonathan came onstage to make the dream a *pas de deux*.

Maddy let her arms come down, then shook them to keep the muscles limber. That was as far as she could go without her partner. Moving to the recorder, she pressed the rewind button. She would do it again.

"I've never seen you dance like that."

Her concentration snapped as she glanced over and saw Reed in the doorway. "Not my usual style." She stopped the squawking tape. "I didn't know you were still around."

"You're a constant amazement," he murmured as he came into the room. "If I didn't know you, I would have looked in here and thought I'd walked in on a prima ballerina."

Though it pleased her, she laughed it away. "A few classic moves isn't Swan Lake."

"But you could do it if you wanted, couldn't you?" He took the towel she held and dabbed at her temples himself.

"I don't know. I'd probably be in the middle of *Sleeping Beauty* and feel an irresistible urge to do a tap routine."

"Ballet's loss is Broadway's gain."

"Keep talking," she said with a laugh. "I need it."

"Maddy, you've been in here nearly two hours. You're going to wear yourself out before curtain."

"Today I have enough energy to do the show three times."

"What about food?"

"Rumor has it the stagehands are fixing goulash. If I pick at some about four or five, I should be able to keep it down during the first act."

"I wanted to take you out."

"Oh, Reed, I couldn't, not before opening night. After." She reached out her hands for his. "We could have a late supper after."

"All right." He felt how cool her hands were even after her dancing. Too cool, too tense. He didn't know how to begin to soothe her. "Maddy, are you always like this before an opening?"

"Always."

"Even though you're confident that it's going to be a hit?"

"Just because I'm confident doesn't mean I don't have to work to make it a hit. And that makes me nervous. Nothing worthwhile happens easily."

"No." His eyes grew more intense on hers. "No, it doesn't."

But they weren't talking about opening nights or about the theater now. His fingers were tense when he spoke again. "You really believe that if you work at something hard enough, believe strongly enough, you can't miss?"

"Yes, I do."

"Us?"

She swallowed. "Yes, us."

"Even though the odds are against it?"

"It isn't a matter of odds, Reed. It's a matter of people."

He dropped her hands and moved away. Just as he had on the paint bridge, he'd felt that quick fear of falling. "I wish I could feel as optimistic as you. I wish I could believe in miracles."

She felt the hope that had ballooned inside her deflate. "So do I."

"Marriage is important to you." He could see her in the glass, small and standing very straight.

"Yes. The commitment. I was raised to respect that commitment, to understand that marriage wasn't an end but a beginning. Yes, it's important."

"It's a contract," he corrected, speaking almost to himself. "A legal one, and not particularly binding. We both know about contracts, Maddy. We can sign one."

She opened her mouth, then very slowly shut it again before she attempted to speak. "I beg your pardon?"

"I said we'll sign one. It's important to you, more important than I had realized. And it doesn't really matter to me. We can get blood tests, a license, and it's done."

"Blood tests." She let out a staggered breath and braced herself on the little table behind her. "A license. Well, that's certainly cutting out the romantic nonsense, isn't it?"

"It's only a formality." Something was moving uneasily in his stomach as he turned back to her. What he was doing was clear. He was closing his own cage door. Why he was doing it was another matter. "I'm not sure of the law, but if we have to we can drive into New York on Monday and take care of it. You can be back for the evening show Tuesday."

"We wouldn't want it to interfere with our schedules," she said quietly. She'd known he would hurt her, but she hadn't known he would quite simply break her heart. "I appreciate the offer, Reed, but I'll pass." She slammed down the button again and let the music come.

"What do you mean?" He took her arm before she could set into position.

"Just what I said. Excuse me, I have to rehearse."

Her voice had never been cold before. Never cold, never flat, as it was now. "You wanted marriage, and I agreed to it. What more do you want, Maddy?"

She jerked away to face him. "More, *much* more than you're willing to give. God, I'm afraid more than you're capable of giving. I don't want a piece of paper, damn you. I don't want you to do me any favors. Okay, Maddy wants to get married, and since I don't really care one way or the other, we'll sign on the dotted line and keep her happy. Well, you can go to hell."

"That's not what I meant." He would have taken her by the shoulders, but she backed away.

"I know what you meant. I know it too well. Marriage is just a contract, and contracts can be broken. Maybe you'd like to put an escape clause in this one so it can be neat and tidy when you're tired of it. No, thank you."

Had it sounded that cold, that...despicable? He was out of his mind. "Maddy, I didn't come up here knowing we'd get into all of this. It just happened."

"Too spontaneous for you?" This time there was sarcasm, another first. "Why don't you go punch up your lines, Reed?"

"What do you want, candlelight and me down on one knee? Aren't we beyond that?"

"I'm tired of telling you what I want." The fire went out of her eyes. They were cool again and, for the first time, aloof. "I have to be onstage in a few hours, and you've done enough for now to make that difficult for me." She pushed the recorder to take the tape back to the beginning again. "Leave me alone, Reed."

She picked up the count and began. She continued to dance when she was alone and the tears started to fall.

Chapter Twelve

As Reed came down into the corridor, he met his father.

"Maddy still upstairs?" Edwin clapped his arms around his son's shoulders. "Just finished talking with the general manager. Seems we're sold out for tonight's performance. In fact, we're sold out through the week. I wanted to tell her."

"Give her a little while." Reed dug his fists into his pockets and struggled against a feeling of utter frustration. "She's working on a routine."

"I see." He thought he did. "Come in here for a minute." He gestured toward the stage manager's office. When they were inside, he shut the door behind them. "You used to tell me when you had problems."

"You get to a point where you'd better know how to solve them yourself."

"You've always been good at that, Reed. It doesn't mean you can't run them by me." He took out a cigar, lighted it and waited.

"I asked Maddy to marry me. No," he went on quickly before the pleasure could dawn in Edwin's eyes. "That's not quite true. I laid out the arrangements for a marriage to Maddy. She tossed them right back at me."

"Arrangements?"

"Yes, arrangements." Reed was defensive, and his voice was sharp and impatient. "We need blood tests, a license; we have to fit it into our schedules."

"It?" Edwin repeated with a slight inclination of his head. "You make it sound very cut-and-dried, Reed. No orange blossoms?"

"She can have a truckload of orange blossoms if she wants them." The room was too small to allow him to storm around it. Instead, he stood where he was and strained against the enforced stillness.

"If she wants them." Understanding too well, Edwin nodded and lowered himself into the one chair. "Reed, if you put marriage on that sort of level with a woman like Maddy, you deserved to have it tossed back at you."

"Maybe I did. Maybe it's for the best. I don't know why I started the whole business."

"It might be because you love her."

"Love's a word that sells greeting cards."

"If I thought you believed that, I'd consider myself a complete failure."

"No." Outraged, Reed turned to him. "You've never failed at anything."

"That's not true. I failed at my marriage."

"Not you." The bitterness rose up, too huge to swallow.

"Yes, I did. You listen to me now. We never talked about this properly. You never wanted to, and I let it go because I felt you'd been hurt enough. I shouldn't have." Edwin looked at his cigar, then slowly crushed it out. "I married your mother knowing she didn't love me. I thought I could keep her bound to me because I could pull the strings to give her what she wanted. The more strings I pulled, the more she felt hemmed in. When she finally broke free, it was as much my fault as hers."

"No."

"Yes," Edwin corrected. "Marriage is two people, Reed. It's not a business, it's not an arrangement. It's not one person wanting to keep the other indebted."

"I don't know what you're talking about," Reed said. "I don't see any reason to get into this now."

"You know there's a reason. She's upstairs right now."

Reed stopped even as he gripped the handle of the door. Slowly he let it go again and turned back. "You're right."

Edwin settled back. "Your mother didn't love me, and she didn't love you. I'm sorry for that, but you should know that love isn't something that comes just from giving birth or just from duty. It comes from the heart."

"She betrayed you."

"Yes. But she also gave you to me. I can't hate her, Reed, and it's time you stopped letting what she did run your life."

"I could be like her."

"Is that what this is about?" Edwin heaved himself up and took Reed by the lapels in the first gesture of violence he'd ever shown his son. "How long have you been carrying this around?"

"I could be like her," Reed repeated. "Or I could be like the man she slept with, and I don't even know who he was."

Edwin loosened his hold and stepped back. "Do you want to know?"

Reed combed both hands through his hair. "No, they're nothing to me. But how can I know what's inside of me? How can I know that what they were wasn't passed on?"

"You can't. But you can look in the mirror and think about who you are and have been, rather than who you might be. And you can believe, as I do, that the last thirty-five years that we've had together is more important."

"I know it is, but—"

"There are no buts."

"I'm in love with Maddy." With the words came a slow shattering of defenses he'd lived with since childhood. "How do I know that won't change next month, next year? How can I know I'm capable of giving her what it is she needs for the rest of our lives?"

"That's something else you can't ever know." Why couldn't the answers be simple ones? It seemed to Edwin that there had never been simple answers for Reed. "That's something you have to risk, something you have to want and something you have to work at. If you love her, you will."

"I'm more afraid of hurting her than I am of anything else. She's the best thing that ever happened to me."

"I don't suppose you mentioned all this when you were outlining the arrangements?"

"No." He rubbed his hands over his face. "I made a mess of it."

"I'd be more concerned if you'd been too smooth."

"You don't have to worry about that. I pushed her away because I was afraid to reach out for her."

Smiling, Edwin rocked back on his heels. "I'll tell you this. No son of mine would let a woman like Maddy O'Hurley slip through his fingers because he thinks he might not be perfect."

After running a hand over his face, Reed nearly laughed. "That sounds like a challenge."

"Damn right it is." Edwin put his hands on Reed's shoulders. "And my money's on you. Remember that game in your senior year? Ninth inning, two outs, the score was tied. You worked the batter to a full count."

"Yeah, I remember." This time he did laugh. "I threw a knuckleball and he knocked it over the fence."

"That's right." Edwin grinned at him. "But it was a hell of a pitch. Why don't you buy your old man a drink?"

With her hair pulled back by a thick band and the rattiest robe she owned tied loosely at the waist, Maddy sat at makeup mirror and carefully attached false lashes to her own. Her makeup was nearly done, and even with one eye lashed and the other naked, she'd already captured the exotic look that was Mary's. Just a little too much color on the cheeks. Just a little too much sparkle on the eyelids, and a rich ripe red for the lips. As she fastened the other lash, she waited for the knot in her stomach to untie itself.

Opening-night nerves, just opening-night nerves, she told herself as she carefully adjusted the liner on her left eye. But there was more than that rushing around inside her, and she couldn't get away from it.

Marriage. Reed had spoken of marriage—but on his terms. The part of her that was always open to hope had waited for the moment when he would accept the fact that they should be together. The part of her that was always willing to see the best of things had been certain that moment would come. Now that it had, she couldn't take it. What he offered wasn't years of joy but a piece of paper that would bind them together legally, leaving nothing to the emotions.

She had too much of it, Maddy told herself. Too much emotion, not enough logic. A logical woman would have accepted Reed's terms and made the best of it. Instead, she was ending things. Maddy stared at her reflection in the lighted mirror. Tonight was a night for beginnings—and a night for endings.

She rose and walked away from the mirror. She'd seen enough of herself.

Outside in the corridor, people were rushing by. She could hear the noise, the nerves, the energy that was opening night. Her dressing room was packed with flowers, dozens of arrangements that doubled themselves in the mirror and crowded the room with scent.

There were roses from Chantel. White ones. Her parents had sent her a clutch of daisies that looked wild and lovely. There was a bowl of gardenias that she had known had come from Trace before she'd looked at the card. It had merely said Break A Leg. She'd wondered briefly how he'd known where and when to send them. Then she'd stopped wondering and had appreciated.

Other arrangements sat here and there, but there were none from Reed. She hated herself for overlooking the beauty of what she had in the quest for what wasn't there.

"Thirty minutes, Miss O'Hurley."

Maddy pressed a hand to her stomach at the call. Thirty minutes left. Why did she have to have Reed dragging at her mind now? She didn't want to go on. She didn't want to go out there tonight to sing and dance and make a theater full of strangers laugh. She wanted to go home and pull down the shades.

There was a quick knock at her door, but before she could answer, her parents poked their heads through. "Can you use a couple of friendly faces?" Molly asked her.

"Oh, yeah." Maddy stretched out her hands to her mother. "I need all I can get."

"The house is filling up." Frank beamed as he looked around the dressing room. There was a star on the door. He couldn't have asked for more for his daughter. "You got standing room only, kiddo."

"Are you sure?"

"Sure I'm sure." Frank patted her hand. "I talked to the general manager myself. He's wearing out the leather on his shoes dancing around."

"He should wait until the curtain calls to do his dancing." Maddy put a hand to her stomach again and wondered if she had any Alka-Seltzer.

"You won't need it when the curtain goes up," Molly commented, reading her daughter easily. "Opening-night jitters, Maddy, or is there something else you want to tell us about?"

She hesitated, but there had never been any secrets between Maddy and her family. "Just that I'm in love with an absolute fool."

"Oh, well." Molly lifted a brow toward Frank. "I know how that is."

"Just a minute now," he began, but was summarily shooed from the room by his wife.

"Out, Frank. Maddy has to get into costume."

"I've powdered her bottom," he muttered, but allowed himself to be pushed out the door. "Knock them dead," he told his daughter. Then he winked and was gone.

"He's terrific, isn't he?" Maddy smiled as she heard him call out to one of the the dancers.

"He has his moments." Molly glanced at the costume of sequins and feathers hanging on the back of the door. "That for opening?"

"Yes."

"I'll give you a hand." Molly took it off the hanger as Maddy tossed her robe aside. "The fool wouldn't happen to be Reed Valentine, would it?"

"That's him." Maddy wiggled herself into the snug bikini.

"We had dinner with him and his father tonight." She helped Maddy hook the brief spangled bra that would go under the outer costume. "Seems like a nice young man."

"He is. I never want to see him again."

"Mm-hmmm."

"Fifteen minutes, Miss O'Hurley."

"I think I'm going to be sick," Maddy whispered.

"No, you're not." With competent hands, Molly pressed the Velcro together at her daughter's hip. "It seemed to me that your Reed was a bit distracted at dinner."

"He's got a lot on his mind." Maddy turned this way and that to be certain the costume was secure. "Contracts, mostly," she added in a mutter. "Anyway, I'm not interested."

"Yes, I can see that. They don't make our lives easier, you know."

"What?"

"Men." Molly turned her daughter around. "They weren't put here to make our lives easier. They were just put here."

For the first time in hours, Maddy felt a laugh bubbling up. "Did you ever think the Amazons had it right?"

"The ones who killed off the men after they'd made love with them?" Molly seemed to consider the question seriously before shaking her head. "No, I don't think so. There's something comforting about having one man for a lifetime. You get used to him. Where are your shoes?"

"Right here." Studying her mother, Molly stepped into them. "You still love Pop, don't you? I mean really, really love him, just the way you always did?"

"No." When Maddy's mouth dropped open, Molly laughed. "Nothing stays the same. The way I love Frank now is different from the way I loved him thirty years ago. We've four children now, and a lifetime of fights and laughter and tears. I couldn't have loved him this much when I was twenty. I doubt I love him as much now as I will when I'm eighty."

"I wish . . ." Maddy let her words trail off, shaking her head.

"No, tell me what you wish." Molly's voice was gentle, as it rarely was. "A daughter can tell her mother anything, especially wishes."

"I wish Reed could understand that. I wish he could see that sometimes it can work, sometimes it can last. Mom, I love him so much."

"Then I'll give you one piece of advice." She took Maddy's wig off the stand. "Don't give up on him."

"I think I'm giving up on me."

"Well, that'll be a first for an O'Hurley. Sit down, girl. Maybe this wig will help keep the brains in your head."

"Thanks."

The five-minute call sounded. Molly walked to the door, then turned to give her daughter one last look. "Don't miss your cue."

"Mom." Maddy rose, keeping her shoulders straight. "I'm going to bring down the house."

"I'm counting on it."

Maddy stepped out of her dressing room with four minutes to spare. A member of the chorus came clattering down the stairs with an outrageous plume of ostrich feathers on her head. The overture was already playing. She walked toward the music, losing a little bit of Maddy O'Hurley with every step. Wanda was already in the wings taking long, cleansing breaths.

"This is it."

Maddy smiled at her before she looked over the stage manager's shoulder to the monitor on his desk. He could watch the play from there, seeing it as the audience did. "What's the top in curtain calls for you, Wanda?"

"We got seventeen in Rochester once."

Maddy put her hands on her hips. "We're going to beat the hell out of that tonight." She walked onstage, faced the curtain and took her mark. As the other dancers filled the stage, she could feel the fear-laced excitement. The nightclub set was in darkness behind her. Hidden by the wings was Macke at stage right. Maddy glanced over at him and tossed her head. She was ready.

"House lights half . . . go."

She drew in oxygen.

"Cue one . . . go."

Above her head, lights flashed on, bathing her in a rainbow.

"House lights off . . . go."

The audience hushed.

"Curtain."

It rose, and so did the music.

By the time Maddy walked off stage right for the first scene change, the electricity was high. Immediately wardrobe began stripping off one costume and bundling her into the next. She breathed a sigh as her wig was removed and her own hair fluffed out.

"You keep that energy up until the final curtain and I'll buy you the best meal in Philadelphia."

Maddy caught her breath as she stared at Macke. Her dress was zipped, her shoes changed and her makeup toned down, all in a matter of two minutes. "You're on." Then she made the dash that would take her under the stage and across for her cue.

She passed beneath the floor of the stage and crossed behind the orchestra pit, where the musicians now were silent. Her Jonathan and the actor who played his best friend were exchanging lines. She heard the audience give a roll of laughter as she moved through a makeshift lounge where enterprising members of the crew had gathered a couple of chairs and a sagging sofa. Near the steps that would lead her back up stage left, a group of stagehands loitered around a small portable television. The sound was down to a low buzz so that the business on stage could be heard clearly. Maddy paused, knowing she had time before the next cue. Obviously they did, too.

"Who's winning?" she asked as she caught a glimpse of the ball game.

"No score. Pirates against the Mets. They're in the third inning."

"My money's on the Mets."

One of the men laughed. "Hope you don't mind losing it."

"Five bucks," she said as she heard Jonathan finishing up his song.

"You're on," he told her.

"I certainly am." She went up the steps and out onstage for her first encounter with Jonathan C. Wiggings III.

The chemistry was right. Mary and Jonathan met on the library steps. They clicked. The audience's interest was caught up in the romance between the stripper and the rich man's son with innocence shining out of his eyes.

The last number before intermission was Maddy's striptease. She came rushing in, as she had in rehearsal, struggling out of her prim dress and into her flamboyant costume and wig. Her dialogue with Wanda was edgy and acerbic, her argument with Terry tough. Then the lights came up in hot pinks and reds. She began with her energy at peak and never let it slide.

She whipped the boa off and let it fly. The audience sent up a howl as it landed in her father's lap.

For you, Pop, she thought as she sent him a broad wink. Because you taught me everything.

Maddy kept her word and brought the house down.

Intermission wasn't a time for relaxing. There were costume changes, makeup to be freshened, energy to be recharged. Word was sent to Maddy that the Mets were down in the sixth, 2-zip. She took it philosophically. She'd lost more important things that day.

From her place in the wings, Maddy sipped a cup of water and peered out at the audience. The house lights were up, and she could see people swarming around the theater. The buzz of excitement was there. She had helped put it there.

Then she saw Reed with the lights from the chandeliers spilling over his hair. Her father stood beside him, inches shorter, years older but just as vital. As she watched, Frank laughed and tossed an arm around Reed's shoulder. It warmed her. She told herself it didn't matter, could no longer matter, but it warmed her to see her father laughing with the man she loved.

Maddy stepped back until the audience was blocked from her view.

"You look like that, you're going to scare them away before the finale."

Turning, Maddy looked at Wanda. They were both dressed in nightclothes for the scene in the apartment they shared. The beaded curtain would come down soon, and Maddy would do her dream sequence. "I can't do that. We still have to beat those seventeen curtain calls."

"He out there?" Wanda didn't bother to look, but motioned with her head.

"Yes, he's there."

The house lights flashed off and on, off and on. Wanda quietly began her deep breathing. "I guess you've got something to prove."

That I can survive, Maddy thought. That I can complete my own life if I have to. "To myself," she murmured before they moved out to their marks. "Not to him, to myself."

In plays, the writer can twist events, shift them, manipulate them to create a happy ending. In the end, Mary and Jonathan had each other. They had overcome differences and deceptions, backgrounds and lies, distrust and disillusionment. For them, happy-ever-after was there for the taking.

Then the applause began. It rolled, it thundered and echoed over the chorus as they took their bows. It continued, only stronger, over the principals. With her hands gripped together, Maddy waited. She would go out last.

With her head up and the smile already in place, Maddy strode out onstage. Applause rose like lava, warm and fluid. The cheers began in the balcony and rolled down, growing louder, still louder, until the theater was filled with them. She took her first bow with them ringing in her head.

Then they were standing, first one, then two, then a dozen. Hundreds of people rose up to their feet and shouted for her. Stunned, she could only stand there and look.

"Take another bow," Wanda said to her in an undertone. "You earned it."

Maddy broke out of her trance and bowed again before linking hands with Wanda and her partner. The cast as a unit bowed again, and the curtain came down. The applause kept coming, wave after wave, as Maddy threw her arms around Wanda and squeezed.

The unity was there, a line of dancers, a group of actors, all of whom had worked and studied and rehearsed endless hours for this one moment. So they held on to it as the curtain, for a moment, cut them off from the audience and ranged them together.

"Here we go again," Maddy said, and locked her hands tight.

The curtain rose and fell twenty-six times.

It took Maddy some time to work her way back to her dressing room. There were people to hug and a few tears to be shed. Macke scooped her up in his arms and kissed her full on the mouth.

"You better be just as damn good tomorrow," he told her.

It was a riot backstage, with dancers whooping around and planning a big celebration. They were a hit. Whatever adjustments, polishing or tightening that would have to be done before Broadway couldn't take away from the fact that they were a hit. No one could take it away from them. The hours and hours of work, sweat and repetition had paid off.

Feet clattered on stairs as members of the chorus scrambled up to their dressing rooms. Someone had a trumpet and was blaring out reveille. Maddy squeezed through the crowd in the hall and into her own room. There she collapsed on a chair and stared at her own reflection.

There were pots and tubes jumbled over the surface of the table. Greasepaint, powder, every color of the rainbow. Above it, she studied her own face, then broke into a grin.

She'd done it.

Her dressing room door opened, and part of the riot slipped in. She saw her father first, the boa slung around his shoulders like a mantle of victory. Energy poured back into her as she jumped out of her chair to fling herself into his arms.

"Pop. It was great. Tell me it was great."

"Great? Twenty-six curtain calls is better than great."

"You counted."

"Of course I counted." He squeezed her hard until her feet left the floor. "That was my girl out there. My baby girl knocking them dead. I'm so proud of you, Maddy."

"Oh, Pop, don't cry." Sniffling herself, she reached into his pocket for a handkerchief. "You'd have been proud of me if I'd flopped." She dried his eyes. "That's why I love you."

"How about a hug for your mother?" Molly held out her arms and gathered Maddy close. "All I could think of was the first time we put you in dance shoes. I could hardly believe it was you, so strong, so vital. Strong." Molly drew her back by the shoulders. "That's what you are, Madeline O'Hurley."

"My heart's still racing." Laughing, Abby embraced her sister. "Every time you came out, I'd grab Dylan's hand. I don't know how many fingers I broke. Ben kept telling the woman beside him you were his aunt. I just wish—"

"I know, I wish Chantel could have been here, too." She leaned down to hug Ben, then glanced up at Chris, who was nestled droopy eyed in Dylan's arms.

"I didn't fall asleep," Chris told her with a huge yawn. "I watched the whole thing. It was pretty."

"Thanks. Well, Dylan, do you think we're ready for Broadway?"

"I think you're going to rock Broadway back on its heels. Congratulations, Maddy." Then he grinned and let his gaze slide down her. "I also liked your costumes."

"Flashy, but brief," she said with a chuckle as she glanced down at the red merry widow she wore.

"We have to get the kids back." Abby looked at Ben. His hand was already caught in Dylan's. "We'll see you tomorrow, before we go. Call me." Abby touched Maddy's arm in a gesture that said everything. "I'll be thinking of you."

"We'll be going, too." Frank sent Molly a sidelong look. "You'll be running out of here to celebrate with the rest of the cast."

"You know you're welcome to come—" Maddy began.

"No, no, we need our rest. We've got a gig in Buffalo in a couple of days. Come on, let's leave the girl to change." Frank nudged his family along, then paused at the door. "You were the best, turnip."

"No." She remembered everything just then—his patience, the joy he'd given to her, the magic he'd passed on when he'd taught her to dance. "You were, Pop."

Maddy sighed and sat again. She drew a rose out of its vase to hold it to her cheek. The best, she thought, shutting her eyes. Why wasn't it enough?

When the door opened again, she straightened in her chair and had her smile ready. Reed stood in the doorway, with noise and confusion reigning behind him. Very carefully Maddy set the rose back in place. The bright smile didn't seem so necessary now.

"Do you mind if I come in?"

"No." But she didn't look at him. Deliberately she turned to the mirror and peeled off her lashes.

"I don't have to tell you how terrific you were." He shut the door on the stream of noise outside.

"Oh, I don't get tired of hearing it." She dipped her hand into a pot of cold cream, then smeared it on. "So you stayed for the show."

"Of course I stayed." She was making him feel like an idiot. He'd never pursued a woman before, not this way. And he knew if he made another mistake he'd lose her for good. When he came up behind her, he saw her hand hesitate, then tremble before she continued to rub in the cream. It eased the tension at the back of his neck. He hadn't lost her yet.

"I guess you know you got your money's worth." Maddy pulled out a tissue and began to wipe off the cream and layers of makeup.

"Yes, I do." He set a large blue box on the table at her elbow. She forced herself to ignore it. "But my father's taking over the show-business side. He wanted me to tell you how much he enjoyed tonight, how incredible he thought you were."

"I though he'd come back."

"He knew I needed to see you alone."

She tossed tissues in the wastebasket. Mary was gone, and there was only Maddy now. Rising, she reached for a robe. "I need to get out of costume. Do you mind?"

"No." He kept his eyes on hers. "I don't mind."

Because she decided he wouldn't make it easy, Maddy simply nodded and moved behind a Chinese screen. "So, you must be going back to New York tomorrow."

"No."

The hooks slipped out from between her fingers. Setting her teeth, Maddy attacked them again. "If your father's taking over, there's no need for you to stay."

"I'm not going anywhere, Maddy. If you want to make me crawl, I guess you're entitled."

She slammed the costume over the screen. "I don't want to make you crawl. That's ridiculous."

"Why? I've been a complete fool. I'm ready to admit it, but if you're not ready to accept it, I can wait."

She yanked the tie on her robe before she came around the screen. "You don't play fair. You've never played fair."

"No, I haven't. And it's cost me." He took a step toward her but saw from the look in her eyes that he could go no farther. "If it means I have to start over, from this point, I'll start over. I want you, Maddy, more than I've ever wanted anything or anyone.''

"Why are you doing this?" She pulled a hand through her hair and looked for a way out. There wasn't one. "Every time I convince myself it's done and over with, every time I say okay, Maddy, give it up, you pull the rug out from under me. I'm tired of falling on my rear end with you, Reed. I just want to find my balance again."

This time he went to her, because nothing could stop him. His eyes were very dark, but she didn't see the panic in them. "I know you can live without me. I know you can shoot right to the top without me. And maybe, just maybe, I can walk away from you and survive. I don't want to risk it. I'll do whatever I can not to."

"Don't you understand, if the foundation isn't there, if we don't understand each other, don't trust each other, it won't ever work? I love you, Reed, but—"

"Don't say anything else." Though she held herself stiff, he drew her close. "Let me hang on to that for a minute. I've done a lot of thinking, a lot of changing, since I met you. Things were pretty black-and-white before you came along. You've added the color, and I don't want to lose that. No, don't say anything," he repeated. "Open the box first."

"Reed—"

"Please, just open the box first." If he knew her as well as he thought, as well as he hoped, that would say more to her than he could.

Strong. Her mother had told her she was strong. She had to believe it now. Maddy turned away and lifted the top on the box. For a moment, she could only stare.

"I didn't send you flowers," Reed began. "I figured you'd have plenty of them. I thought—I hoped—this would mean more. Hannah had a hell of a time getting it up here."

Speechless, Maddy lifted the plant out. When she'd given it to him, it had been soggy and yellowed and already rotting away. Now it was green and vivid, with strong young shoots. Because her hands were unsteady, she set it down on the table.

"A minor miracle," Reed murmured. "It didn't die when it should have. It just kept fighting, just kept thriving. You can make miracles happen if you want them badly enough. You told me that once, and I didn't believe it. I do now." He touched her hair and waited until she looked back at him. "I love you. All I want is for you to give me a lifetime to prove it."

She stepped into his arms. "Start now."

With laughter and relief he brought his lips to hers and felt the welcome. She drew him closer with a sigh, holding on with all the love, all the strength, she would promise him.

"I never had a chance," he murmured. "Not from the first minute I saw you. Nothing, thank God, has been the same for me since." But he drew her away, needing to pass the last hurdle. "Those things I said this afternoon—"

Placing a finger over his lips, she shook her head. "You're not going to try to back out of marrying me now."

"No." He held her close again, then let her go. "No, but I can't ask you until you know everything about me." It was hard, harder than he'd thought it could be. He let his hands drop away from her. "Maddy, my father..."

"Is an exceptional man," she finished for him, taking his hand. "Reed, he told me everything weeks ago."

"He told you?"

"Yes." She reached up to soothe the tension before it could form. "Did you think it would make a difference?"

"I couldn't be sure."

She shook her head. Rising on her toes, she kissed him again, letting the love pour out. "Be sure. There's no candlelight," she pointed out. "And I don't want you to get down on one knee. But I do want you to ask me."

He took both of her hands, and as he brought them to his lips, his eyes never left her. "I love you, Maddy. I want to spend my life with you, have children with you, take chances with you. I want to sit in the front row and watch you explode on the stage and know when it's over you'll come home to me. Will you marry me?"

The smile came slowly, until it lighted her whole face. She opened her mouth, then let out a groan as a sharp knock sounded at her door.

"Get rid of them," Reed demanded.

Maddy gave his hands a quick squeeze. "Just don't move. Don't even breathe." She yanked the door open, prepared to shut it again just as quickly.

"Your five, Miss O'Hurley." One of the stagehands grinned at her and offered her a bill. "Mets took it 4–3. Looks like you just can't lose tonight."

She took the bill and ran it through her hands. Looking over her shoulder, she smiled at Reed. "You're so right."

* * * * *

The O'Hurleys—united at last!
Look for THE LAST HONEST WOMAN,
DANCE TO THE PIPER, SKIN DEEP
and WITHOUT A TRACE
coming out this month—
only in Silhouette Special Edition.

FOUR UNIQUE SERIES
FOR EVERY WOMAN YOU ARE . . .

Silhouette Romance

Love, at its most tender, provocative,
emotional . . . in stories that will make you laugh and
cry while bringing you the magic of falling in love.

6 titles per month

Silhouette Special Edition

Sophisticated, substantial and packed with
emotion, these powerful novels of life and love will
capture your imagination and steal your heart.

6 titles per month

SILHOUETTE *Desire*

Open the door to romance and passion. Humorous,
emotional, compelling—yet always a believable
and sensuous story—Silhouette Desire never
fails to deliver on the promise of love.

6 titles per month

Silhouette Intimate Moments

Enter a world of excitement, of romance
heightened by suspense, adventure and the
passions every woman dreams of. Let us
sweep you away.

4 titles per month

Double your reading pleasure this fall with two Award of Excellence titles written by two of your favorite authors.

Available in September

DUNCAN'S BRIDE
by Linda Howard
Silhouette Intimate Moments #349

Mail-order bride Madelyn Patterson was nothing like what Reese Duncan expected—and everything he needed.

Available in October

THE COWBOY'S LADY
by Debbie Macomber
Silhouette Special Edition #626

The Montana cowboy wanted a little lady at his beck and call—the "lady" in question saw things differently....

These titles have been selected to receive a special laurel—the Award of Excellence. Look for the distinctive emblem on the cover. It lets you know there's something truly wonderful inside! DUN-1

Silhouette Special Edition

Now appearing
in a special return engagement, Nora Roberts's
bestselling 1988 miniseries featuring

THE O'HURLEYS!
Nora Roberts

Book 1 THE LAST HONEST WOMAN *Abby's Story*
Book 2 DANCE TO THE PIPER *Maddy's Story*
Book 3 SKIN DEEP *Chantel's Story*

And making his debut in a brand-new title, a very special
leading man . . . Trace O'Hurley!

Book 4 WITHOUT A TRACE *Trace's Tale*

In 1988, Nora Roberts introduced THE O'HURLEYS!—a close-knit
family of entertainers whose early travels spanned the country. The
beautiful triplet sisters and their mysterious brother each experience
the triumphant joy and passion only true love can bring, in four books
you will remember long after the last pages are turned.

Don't miss this captivating miniseries—a special collector's edition
available now wherever paperbacks are sold.

OHUR-1A